The Disciple

The Disciple

*To Denise
with love*

K. Holmes

Ken Holmes

Copyright © 2014 Ken Holmes

The moral right of the author has been asserted.

Apart from any fair dealing for the purposes of research or private study, or criticism or review, as permitted under the Copyright, Designs and Patents Act 1988, this publication may only be reproduced, stored or transmitted, in any form or by any means, with the prior permission in writing of the publishers, or in the case of reprographic reproduction in accordance with the terms of licences issued by the Copyright Licensing Agency. Enquiries concerning reproduction outside those terms should be sent to the publishers.

Matador
9 Priory Business Park,
Wistow Road, Kibworth Beauchamp,
Leicestershire. LE8 0RX
Tel: (+44) 116 279 2299
Fax: (+44) 116 279 2277
Email: books@troubador.co.uk
Web: www.troubador.co.uk/matador

ISBN 978 1783065 462

British Library Cataloguing in Publication Data.
A catalogue record for this book is available from the British Library.

Typeset in 11pt Adobe Garamond Pro by Troubador Publishing Ltd, Leicester, UK
Printed and bound in the UK by TJ International, Padstow, Cornwall

Matador is an imprint of Troubador Publishing Ltd

Captured by a moment in time
A prisoner to the mystery of her smile
I must re-create it in order to be free
But I am not Michaelangelo
But then Michaelangelo could not do it either
He was not there
Nobody was, except me

CONTENTS

PART 1:   THE HOLIDAY   1

PART 2:   THE WILDERNESS   107

PART 3:   THE ORACLE   203

PART 1

THE HOLIDAY

Chapter 1

Molly put the phone down. "Damn!! Bloody… bloody hell!"

Her mother looked up, expressionless.

"He's going to be late!"

Molly turned towards the door. "Come down a minute, love… I need you to go to the chippy."

She turned back to her mother, "Some bloody machine's broken down or something. I bloody knew this would happen! SINEAD!!! Machine's broken down… I bet he's got time for the pub!"

If you knew this was going to happen, why all the fuss thought her mother, but she kept it as a thought.

"I asked him to do one thing… one bloody thing!" as she went upstairs.

In a different life, Daisy, Molly's mother, would be sitting on a rocking chair on a verandah in some distant Mississippi backwater, and that's where she spends most of her time since Harry died.

"I'll call you back," Sinead put the phone down as her mother walked in. She'd been crying.

"What's the matter, love?" Molly sat on the bed beside her daughter and put her arm round her. "Was that Terry?"

She nodded.

"It's only ten days, love. He's going to love you all the more when we get back."

"I don't want to go."

"Now don't be silly. You were all for it yesterday. We were laughing, weren't we. Now dry your eyes and wipe your face – I need you to go to the chippy."

"I don't want to go, Mam. I want to stay here."

"Now look, love, don't be silly – you can't stay here. Your Dad was going to bring in some fish and chips so I can carry on with the packing, but he's got to work late – and now JJ's just got mud all over his new trainers, so I need your help. Will you go to the chippy for us?"

"Can't JJ go?"

"Yeah, I'll go, Mam," chipped in JJ, listening at the door. "I'll get some of those crispies – they're free if the fat man's there."

"No, you can't, you can't go on your own… and I'm talking to Sinead. You can both go, though."

"No, I'll go by myself, if I've got to go."

"Aah! Why can't I go?"

"Cos you're a pain!"

"Well, get some of them crispies, then."

"Are these all your clothes, love, at the end of the bed – and those few on the sideboard?"

Sinead nodded.

"Come on then, get to the chippy, and we'll get the packing finished. 'Cos we want to make sure everything's ready tonight, don't we, so we've got no panicking in the morning."

Sinead nodded. "Yeah, I'm sorry, Mam."

"Don't be sorry. It wasn't that long ago, you know… I know what it's like. Let's have our tea, finish the packing, and then you can phone him back… Look at the state of your trainers – they're black!"

"Just a bit of dirt, Mam. You've got to break them in."

"I'll break you in in a minute! Now get downstairs and take them off."

In the Duck House, Jimmy and Billy walked in, ordered a couple of pints and sat down.

Jimmy looked at his cool pint of lager, "I'm going to murder that."

"Well, it's all done now, Jimmy lad. This time tomorrow…"

"Yeah, ten days of sun, sea and… What do they drink in Corfu… Pina Coladas? No, it's that ouzo, isn't it?"

"Yeah, lighter fuel – send you to the funny farm, that stuff."

"Anyway, have you packed yet?"

"Yeah, more or less. Take me five minutes. Did Molly kick off when you told her you were working late?"

"Oh, she pretended to. Funny woman. You know, when I'm home she tells me to get out 'cos she gets nothing done, and then when I've got to work late she kicks off. Funny breed, women, aren't they? But you've got to love them. Ten days of bikinis, Billy lad! They go topless there, don't they?"

"Topless? All of it!"

"Do they?"

"No idea."

Chapter 2

Now about that time, God, the Big Guy up in heaven, was having one of those rare moments when he could sit down, relax, and catch up with the newspapers, but he didn't stay relaxed for long; in fact he was getting just about as far from relaxed as it's possible to get.

"Enough!" he roared, not like a lion would roar – it was more like an inner roar. Nevertheless it was enough to rattle the cage and everybody in it. He summoned all the archangels – in a godly fashion, you understand – and told them he was becoming decidedly pissed off (he didn't actually use that word, but it's the nearest one we've got in translation; 'upset', 'disgruntled', 'fed up', just didn't do it – he was pissed off) – with a world that was becoming increasingly corrupt with the lust for money, for wealth and material things… and worse.

"It's just as bad now," he told them, "as it was two thousand years ago when the lad, young Jesus, was running round Galilee, and it's not the way.

"So," he said to the hushed gathering, "here's the plan."

"A plan… A plan?" one or two repeated in hushed tones, then total silence – you could have heard a gossamer wing drop. Everybody waited in nervous anticipation. They hadn't had a plan since… when was it? Noah's boat thing… that was a plan… and the parting of the Red Sea – that was a cracker.

"We are going," the Big Guy continued, "We are going to have a new disciple."

"Wow!!!" The shock of what they had just heard rocked the very foundations of heaven. Not literally, of course, as the foundations of heaven as everybody knows are based on truth, honesty and eternal peace, love – all that sort of stuff – and not, well… rockable.

After an age, or more like several ages, some of the archangels began murmuring as to what he actually meant by 'disciple'. I mean, they knew the literal definition of 'disciple' but this was more than that. They all knew that much.

No-one would have dared say, but they were all thinking, he did mention the Jesus word, and everybody knows he was actually the son of the Big Guy.

Was he actually thinking…? Can he? Can he still? The last time was…

But just before they got into deep do-do he continued, "One of you is going to create the new disciple."

"What!!!"

"What!!!"

"What a mind you lot have got! I'm not talking about immaculate conception!"

There was a deep sigh of relief from them all, apart from the tangible disappointment of about three or four, the usual suspects, who thought they'd won the lottery.

"So," he went on, "things are going to change. We're going to look at the radical alternative, because all our representatives on earth are just as bad – devious and greedy as all the rest." After a moment's thought, he corrected himself, "No, not all… In fact most of them are decent chaps and chapesses – but they're letting the evil few within the churches get away with it, and that's nearly as bad.

"I've just been reading about more cases of paedophilia and child abuse within the Church, and it's gone on for years. I was aware of it, of course, but the point is so were they. There must have been thousands who knew all this was going on, and did nothing.

"So… we – that's the royal We, you understand, which means you – are going to come up with a radical alternative, a new… disciple."

There were gasps all round.

"… and come up with it by Tuesday."

I think I should point out at this stage that you should not take this as a literal translation because, for instance, Tuesday does not exist in heaven as an indication of a particular day. Time past and future do not exist either; there is just a permanent present. But it's difficult to explain this concept. Neither would he refer to his archangels as 'you lot', but it is perhaps the best way to illustrate the mood of the big guy, who was letting them know in no uncertain manner that he was kicking celestial arse.

They all dispersed in a buzz of excitement, and began to form small groups to decide best procedure, some discussing what the Big Guy meant by 'radical' and how radical were they meant to be, and what did radical mean anyway.

Others decided to start celebrating in advance. A new disciple was big stuff, the biggest thing since a good number of the younger archangels had gained their super-deluxe wings.

Archangel Voice was never one to pass up the opportunity for a good shindig, and was probably one of the most radical of all the archangels. Well, to say he'd had a few slurps of moon juice was a bit of an understatement: he was as spaced out as the giggle monkeys on Pluto. It was during that altered state that he became inspired, and selected…

Chapter 3

"Is that our plane, Dad? Is it, Dad? Is that our plane?"

It was nine-thirty the following morning, and they had arrived at the airport. Molly and Jimmy Downie, Molly's mother Daisy, and the two kids, Sinead, sixteen, and Jimmy Junior, or JJ, nearly ten – and Jimmy's mate, Billy.

A jet was making its approach. "Is that our plane, Dad?"

Jimmy stared into the sky.

"Probably lad… Cosmic." His mind was way beyond the planes.

"What's cosmic, Mam?"

"That's best known to yer Dad. Here lad, come here. Help me carry this."

There was an air of nervous anticipation as they approached the entrance. None of them had been abroad before, or on a plane before, apart from Sinead who went to Switzerland with school two years ago, but that gave her the edge over the others.

"Right, we have to look for the big board with all the departures on… there it is…" But that was as far as she got. Her voice stopped mid-sentence. Then everything went black, jet black, just for a moment. When the light returned, the airport was still, silent, frozen in time, as if someone had pressed the pause button… apart from Jimmy.

He nudged Molly, "What the hell was that?"

But she couldn't hear him, didn't move, frozen like a statue looking at Sinead. Sinead was the same, pointing towards the departures board. He saw a man in uniform, a pilot. He walked over, "What was all that about?" But nothing. The whole airport was still, silent, nothing and nobody moved.

Then he heard a noise, a voice, a whisper, quiet, as though not to disturb anyone, "Jimmy Downie."

He looked around to see where it came from.

"Jimmy. Jimmy Downie," the whisper grew louder.

It appeared to be coming from above, but it could have been from anywhere.

"Jimmy!" The whisper louder still, a bit impatient.

"Hello?" said Jimmy, nervously.

"At last! Jimmy Downie – You are THE DISCIPLE."

"What?"

Everything went black again, then the light and the hubbub returned and normal service resumed.

"What?" Jimmy repeated.

"Hot? Yeah, it will be," said Molly, "It's Corfu. Anyway, there's the board… let's go and see."

"What the hell just happened?"

"Don't leave the cases there, Jimmy," shouted Molly.

"What the hell was that all about?" But nobody was listening. Jimmy picked up the cases and followed, his head swivelling around trying to find some sort of explanation, trying to make sense of what had just happened. But, nothing, apart from somewhere in the distance he could hear the Beatles' song, 'Boy, You're Going to Carry That Weight a Long Time'.

"There we are, Check-in Desks numbers 34 to 38. That way." Sinead was feeling quite proud of herself, taking control, "Come on."

"Well, that's not too bad, Jimmy lad," said Billy, as they joined the queue.

"Yeah, it's alright, I think," but he was still trying to figure out what the hell had just happened.

"Do they 'ave Stella in Corfu, Dad?"

"Shurrup."

"Ah, come on, Dad, do they?"

Jimmy scowled.

JJ muttered, "I could murder a pint of Stella."

Jimmy turned to JJ to shut him up, but Molly interjected.

"Leave him alone, Jimmy. He's only excited about our holiday."

They checked all their cases in and got their tickets.

* * *

"Can we go and have a look at the Duty Free, Mam?"

"OK, love, sure. We've got an hour and a half – well, nearly two hours actually."

"Take him with you, will yer. He's doing me head in."

"Oh, alright. Where are you two going?"

"Me and Billy'll go and have a cup of tea over there in that Prat Manager."

"Oh God, Mam. He's going to show us up." Sinead turned to her dad. "It's not Prat Manager, Dad. It's Prêt à Manger. It's French, it means…" she struggled to remember what it did mean.

"I know what it means; it means that's where they manage the prats. And a good job, too."

"It's Prêt à Manger," Sinead repeated, louder. Jimmy stared at the sign, trying to make it read what Sinead had just said, but it wasn't happening.

Molly, Gran and Sinead made their way to the Duty Free shop.

"Come on, Gran," Sinead linked her arm.

"What's a prat manager, Mam?"

"I think I am half the time."

Gran, Molly's mother, lived with them. She moved in four years ago when Harry died, so she wouldn't be lonely and start fretting.

But Gran was a loner, in a way. She seldom spoke, apart from the odd 'hello/goodbye'. She could go days without speaking, unless she had to when going to the shops or on the bus. One time Sinead and JJ decided to see how long Gran could go without speaking, but got into an argument over whether they had started on the Saturday or the Sunday, which developed into a full-blown fight, and they didn't speak to each other for a week, making the house blissfully peaceful.

Molly knew her mam didn't like talking very much because she missed the Old Man – which wasn't strictly true. Molly's mum and dad were far closer than anyone really knew. Over the years they'd developed their own language, a kind of private way of communicating, and any talk outside that was mostly rubbish. She didn't realise how much rubbish people actually talked until Harry died and, rather than contribute to the verbal diarrhoea, she decided to shut up. If people wanted to put that down as fretting, it was OK, but really it was just a flag of convenience.

"What're yer getting from the Duty Free, Mam? Are yer getting some of that Southern Comfort?"

"We're not getting anything, Jimmy J, we're just going to have a look. We've got an hour and a half before we get on the plane so we're just going to have a look at the stuff – and shurrup about Southern Comfort."

"Are, hey, Mam – it's good, Southern Comfort."

* * *

Jimmy and Billy settled down with their pot of tea. Jimmy, deep in thought, leaned towards Billy, "You know when we first came in? Over there, was it? No, over there."

"Over there, yeah. Why are you whispering?"

"When we first came in, did you keep moving, or did you stop?"

"What're you talking about, Jimmy?"

"You know when we first came in, did you keep…?"

"I know when we came in. It was only half an hour ago. We came in, and then we walked over to the Departures thing."

"Well, we didn't, did we. It all went black, didn't it. Then the lights came on again, but everybody was frozen still and it was dead quiet, but I could move. That's what I'm talking about… Now, could you move?" Jimmy was raising his voice with exasperation.

Billy just stared back.

"... and then the voice boomed out *Jimmy Downie – you are a trifle.*"

"Well you've got that right. Have you been drinking the Ambre Solaire?"

"Hang on a mo," Jimmy had spotted two girls walking towards the cafe and his mind clicked in to the main point of the holiday. "Hang on, Billy boy, hang on a minute."

"What's up, Jimmy?"

Jimmy, whispering through gritted teeth, said, "Just hang on a minute, and look casual. See those two birds over there?" Jimmy nodded over his left shoulder. Billy looked. "Don't look, Billy! You've gorra be dead casual. Those two birds are going to Corfu."

"How d'you know that?"

"They were in the check-in behind us. Eh, I tell you what, Billy boy, this is gonna be a great holiday. I bet yer those two birds are bang at it."

"How d'you work that out, Jimmy?"

"You can tell, Billy boy... cat's away, and all that stuff. But you mustn't be too keen, though. You've gorra be dead casual. Pretend we haven't seen them."

The two girls walked past without a second look.

"I don't fancy yours."

Chapter 4

Jimmy and Billy had been best mates for four years, ever since Billy joined Madden's Boxes, though they knew each other well before that.

Jimmy got Billy the job, even though Charlie Madden was not at all sure, but he agreed to take Billy on trial. That was severely tested after one week when Billy crashed the fork-lift truck causing a thousand pounds' worth of damage. Jimmy took the blame, but Charlie knew. Of course he did. But he had a lot of time for Jimmy. Whenever the orders were overloaded or a machine broke down, Jimmy was there. In the early days fifteen years ago, Jimmy had worked with Charlie right through the night to get orders finished. Anyway, Billy had been there four years, now, and drove the fork-lift truck better than Jimmy. They went to the same pubs together and, of course, the match on Saturday.

Billy was still single – not surprising. Going down the Duck House a couple of times a week, and Anfield on a Saturday, isn't exactly the environment to pull women. He'd had the odd girlfriend and, at thirty, nine years younger than Jimmy, he was hardly over the hill.

Jimmy had been planning this holiday for a while, and one of the targets was to show Billy how to pull women. Not that Jimmy was interested in pulling women; he was a happily married man. No, Jimmy was not interested in pulling women. Not much.

* * *

"Oh look, Sinead. They've got some of that Calvin Klinn stuff. I've got some of this Calvin Klinn." Molly picked up a tester and tried it, "Jesus! My Calvin Klinn's better than this."

"It's Calvin Klein, Mam."

"God! Look at the price! It's cheaper than that down the market. I paid half that for my Calvin Klinn."

"It's Calvin Klein, Mam."

"Calvin Klein, Calvin Klinn – it's all the same. It says Calvin Klinn on my one."

"You've heard of Calvin Klein, haven't you, Mam?"

"Yes, of course I have."

"Well that stuff at the market is not Calvin Klein; it's just trying to copy it, but it's not the same."

"Oh right, I see what you mean. I've heard about that. Hey, gits, aren't they! The boxes look identical."

Jimmy J was busy rearranging some of the merchandise. Then he'd found a Liverpool scarf and was putting it on the life-size model on the Estée Lauder stand.

Gran was sitting down by the far wall. The staff had brought a chair that they saved for the frail and elderly. Gran was neither, but she knew how to milk a situation. It was a good vantage point to see everything that was going on.

Jimmy J stood back to admire his work. It needed more. He found a Liverpool shirt – number eight, Stevie G's. He took the shirt back to the Estée Lauder model, and thought deeply, looking around furtively to see if anyone was watching. Now, if the people who designed the model knew at some stage it would be expected to be fitted with a Liverpool football shirt they might have designed it slightly differently, but they hadn't envisaged that eventuality, so in a way they've got to take some of the blame. Sure enough, it crashed to the ground, which caused a big commotion in the Duty-Free. The manager came over and led Jimmy J back to his mother.

"Oh, I'm awful sorry. He's not normally like this. I'm awful sorry. He's just a bit excited. We're going on our holiday, you know – we're going to Corfu."

Now, Gran, who sees all, had a stomach condition, which meant she could break wind from time to time and emit the most foul smell. She had tablets which cured the condition perfectly – when she remembered to take them – though she had greater control over this condition than she cracked on.

Back at the cafe, the two girls had finished their coffee and walked past the lads, chatting, laughing – totally oblivious to our two Lotharios.

"You're wasting your time there, Jimmy lad."

"Early days, Billy. Early days."

"I bet they'll be interested when you've turned into a trifle."

"You did hear that, didn't you? You did hear it."

"No, not exactly."

"Well, what d'you mean 'not exactly'? Did you hear it or not?" Their voices were becoming raised.

"No!"

"Well, what did you say not exactly for then?"

"'Cos you're behaving like a pudding."

The conversation stopped as an angry Molly arrived dragging Jimmy J, with Sinead and Gran following behind.

"Jesus! That lad of yours, Jimmy!"

"What's happened?"

"He's only gone and got us thrown out the Duty-Free… God! The holiday's not started yet, and we've been banned out of the Duty-Free. How many people can say that!"

"What the hell did he do?"

"He's only wrecked the Estée Lauder stand!"

"I didn't wreck it, Dad! It just fell over a bit. I was just trying to put a Liverpool scarf on it and make her look a bit more cool. And then I tried to put the shirt on it and that's when it fell over a bit… and that was all it was."

Jimmy and Billy burst out laughing.

"It's not funny, you two. I never felt so ashamed in all me life!"

"Ah, you shouldn't have done that, lad." Jimmy tried unsuccessfully to look serious.

"It was Stevie G, Dad!"

"Was it?"

"Oh God! I knew I'd get no support from you! And what's this about Southern Comfort he's been on about? Have you been giving him Southern Comfort?"

"I didn't say anything, Dad! I didn't snitch on you. I wouldn't snitch on you."

Back at the Duty-Free, two staff members were rebuilding the Estée Lauder stand; an area over by the far wall had been sectioned off and was being sprayed with what looked like air freshener. No wonder some Scousers get a bad name.

"Oh leave it alone, Mam!"

"Alright. Well there's no harm done, Moll. I think it's time we got to the gate, isn't it, Sinead? What number was it?"

He put his arm round his daughter's shoulder and led the way. "Numbers thirty-four to thirty-eight, was it?"

"No, that was the check-in desk, Dad."

"I know," he whispered to her. "I know the gate as well – it's B9."

She looked at her dad, surprised.

"Just a bit of insurance, love. I knew you wouldn't forget the time, but your mam had a lot of sorting out to do to get us lot up here, and I know sometimes when she gets near the shops it can wipe her slate clean."

"You're not that daft, are you, Dad?"

"A bit of both, kid. Down there for dancing, up here for thinking."

He turned to the others, "Gate B9," he shouted, "plenty of time – no rush.

"He's not a bad lad, you know, your kid brother."

"No, I know. He just takes after you too much."

"Me? You cheeky sod!"

"Yeah – he worships the ground you walk on."

"Well we'd better give him something to copy, then, hadn't we," and they carried on towards the gate – skipping.

* * *

That short walk and talk with Sinead hit Jimmy like a brick. He'd missed the last couple of years of his daughter growing up. He was always there, but Molly looked over her, and she was always with Terry, her boyfriend. So Jimmy was a bit, not superfluous, but not exactly essential either. When they got to the gate, Jimmy had a chat with Molly about the seating.

When they had checked in, the best seats they could get were three pairs, near each other, but not exactly in a row. The arrangement was Jimmy and Billy, Molly and JJ, Gran and Sinead. They rearranged the seating so Jimmy sat next to Sinead, for part of the flight anyway. Billy didn't mind sitting next to JJ, in fact they spent half the time laughing at something or other. They were near enough for Molly to pass out the snacks to keep them going until the food arrived.

After they had settled down, Sinead brought out her book on Corfu. She flicked through the pages, stopping every now and then to read a page or two of the text that went with the pictures.

JJ and Billy were laughing about something, Molly was deep in conversation. Jimmy felt a bit choked at it all. A holiday's about eyeing the talent during the day and getting drunk at night, isn't it? Isn't it?

Chapter 5

It was mid-afternoon when they touched down. They knew it was going to be hot, very hot, but it didn't prepare them for what hit them when they stepped out of the plane. It was like the oven door opening. Neither were they prepared for the Terminal chaos; it seemed like thousands of people with trolleys and suitcases, all in a hurry to get where they were going, and apparently all knowing where that was, except our gang, and where our gang needed to get to was the opposite way to everybody else.

"Everybody stay together!" screeched Molly, "We're in Corfu now." No harm in stating the obvious at times like this. "Are you listening, JJ?"

"I'm here, Mam – I'm not doing nothing."

They stood by the carousel and waited with nervous anticipation as one by one their cases arrived. *First crisis averted*, thought Jimmy.

Then the holiday rep told them, "Coach number seven in row D."

Second crisis averted. They found coach number seven and clambered aboard.

"D'you see what I see, Billy?" said Jimmy through clenched teeth. "Them birds from the airport… they're getting on our coach."

"Go away!"

"Yeah, I think so. Look – I can see them. They're putting their luggage in the whatsaname."

Jimmy gave the two girls the reassuring smile of the seasoned traveller as they passed down the aisle. They missed it.

"Early days, Jimmy," said Billy.

"Are you taking the piss? What a coincidence, though, hey? How many coaches were there – twenty, twenty-five? That's more than a coincidence."

Eight stops, and theirs was number seven. Two hours on the bus – they never reckoned on that. Time passed eventually for our now weary travellers.

Molly leaned over. "Ours is the next stop, I think… JJ's asleep."

"They're still on, Billy," Jimmy whispered. "I tell you, it's destiny."

But the girls were still on when stop number seven came. It was just our gang and one more family getting off for Nikolas' Apartments. Molly, trying to be matter of fact, "Oh, this is nice! Look at all them flowers."

"They're hibiscus."

Sinead flicked through her book. "No, they're not, Dad. They're bougainvillea. Those are hibiscus over there."

"That's right. They're the ones."

Two one-bedroom apartments with a bed-settee in the living room, a sink and a small cooker in the corner, and a shower room with toilet. No wardrobe as such in the bedroom, just a few hooks and a rail with hangers fixed to the wall, and a curtain, but – what the hell – they were in Corfu. The girls in one apartment, and the boys in the other.

"We're going down to find the bar, Molly," shouted Jimmy.

"Well, get us half a lager. No, hang on a mo – I'm just going to stick a few things on hangers – I'll see when I come down. We'll be down in five minutes."

The lads went down to where the bar was, but it was shut. Nobody there. They wandered outside to see where the next bar was, but there wasn't one. There wasn't one of anything.

Jimmy looked up and down the track. "God, where the hell

are we?" Even JJ was quiet. They were still standing staring towards a distant goat when the girls arrived.

"Look at this, they've dropped us off on the moon, and the bar's shut."

"Well, we've been having a chat. The bar'll be open in about an hour, about half five – and it's not a bar, it's more of a restaurant. We've just been talking to… what's her name, Sinead?"

"Despina."

"Yes, Despina. She's very nice. Though her English is about as good as my Greek. But the fellah told us there's a bar just about ten minutes' walk… that way, was it? Or was it that way? Anyway, you two go and find the bar. We'll wait here. I think it's lovely."

"Can I go and find the bar, mam?"

"No, you wait here. You look shattered… Oh, alright, go on then." JJ ran off after his dad.

* * *

An hour and two pints later, Jimmy's faith in humanity was restored, and they were back at Nikolas'.

"We found the sea, Mam. It's dead good! There's people in it. I wanted to go in, didn't I, Dad? But we're going to go in the sea tomorrow, aren't we, Dad?"

"Right," said Molly, "that's great. We'll all go tomorrow. Well, we found out a bit more. Despina's actually Nikolas' wife, and there is a Nikolas. He actually owns this lot. Though there's only five apartments, and we've got two. We've nearly filled half the place. That must be Nikolas over there, see – through the whatsisname. I don't know whether Nikolas does the cooking, but it's his restaurant. I've had a look at the menu – it looks very nice. I reckon we eat here tonight. What d'you think? Despina might be the waitress. She does speak quite good English, actually, doesn't she, Sinead."

Sinead nodded to her dad.

"I'm surprised she's had the opportunity."

* * *

Seven-thirty the next morning, and Jimmy was trying to get everybody out for an early morning swim, but it was eight o'clock before Jimmy, Billy, Sinead and JJ got out.

Molly shouted, "We'll go and find a shop and get something for breakfast.'

Four other people were already in the sea. "Oh, look at that! We're not the first!"

"Doesn't matter, Dad," JJ ran into to sea.

There was a family tradition: when they went to the baths on a Sunday they had to 'splash the pool'. That had to be done at all costs. But today they weren't the first, they were… well, it doesn't matter – you either splash the pool or you don't.

On the way back they passed a taverna with three or four locals sitting outside.

"Can we get a Coke, Dad?"

"No. Though I wouldn't mind a coffee, but I haven't brought any money. Have you got any money, Billy?"

"No. It's in the room."

The man in the taverna heard them. "If you want coffee, please… sit down. You can pay me later."

Jimmy looked at Billy, "Why not?"

They sat down and looked at the list. "Here you are, Jimmy. Look at this: Greek coffee. Are you going to have one?"

"Are you?"

"Me? No. I've heard about that."

"Well I am. When in Rome…"

The waiter came over, "Two coffees, please. I'll have the Greek one."

"Are you sure?" he asked, smiling.

"Yeah, of course I am. Why? What's wrong with it?"

"Oh, nothing."

"And two glasses of orange. Is that OK, Sinead?"

"Yes, please."

"Are hey, Dad! I wanna Coke."

"You'll have orange. It's too early in the day for Coke."

The waiter returned with the drinks, including a glass of water for Jimmy. The locals at the nearby tables started laughing as Jimmy stared at the mud in the bottom of his cup.

"Has he just got that off the beach?" He took a sip, "Christ! How can anybody drink that?"

"Oh, go and get yerself a proper coffee, Dad."

"No! Greek coffee I ordered, and I'm gonna drink it."

Everybody was laughing including the locals at the horror on Jimmy's face as the coffee went down.

"You should have seen the coffee Dad got, Mam!" as they got back to Niko's. JJ ran outside and came back with a handful of soil. "It was just like that!"

"I thought you didn't have any money? I've got it, haven't I? You, go and throw that back outside and wash your hands. We're having breakfast."

"I didn't. The fellah said we can pay him later. He's right, though – the Greek coffee's just like mud."

"He didn't let me have a Coke, Mam. I had to have orange juice."

"Good Lord!" Molly looked at Jimmy, surprised. "Wonders will never cease… Have you washed your hands?"

"No, Mam, they're not dirty – we've just been in the sea."

They had some ham and bread rolls for breakfast – probably the best ham and bread they'd ever had.

* * *

It all seemed kind of surreal as they made their way back down to the beach. Gone was the moon landscape from the previous afternoon, replaced by... Well, the lizard crawling over the rock and pausing for the camera, turning his head to make sure Sinead got his best side; Gran standing nose to nose with the donkey, engaging in some sort of spiritual conversation; and who in their wildest dreams would have thought Jimmy would be stopping to look at the flowers, and then looking in Sinead's book to identify them?

Gran had been in Molly and Jimmy's house for just twelve months now. It wasn't a big house – a three bedroomed terrace. They'd talked about doing up the loft. The Council had done this before to some houses nearby. That would make a good studio pad for Sinead, and Gran could have her room. But they weren't sure how Gran staying with them would work out. She was perfectly healthy; she didn't need looking after, apart from the stomach thing... the bloody stomach thing. So they decided to do the front parlour just as a sort of bedsit, but she had all her meals with the family. The only time the front parlour was used otherwise was at Christmas, though Sinead had been spending hours in there with Terry, her boyfriend, which Jimmy was not at all sure about. Then what would happen if they did the loft up?

Jimmy and JJ went on ahead to pay for the drinks they'd had earlier. The guy in the taverna smiled broadly as Jimmy approached, but he wouldn't take the money. "No, have that one with me."

"That was good of him, wasn't it, Dad?"

"Yes, lad, it was – though there's bound to be a kind of competition with the tavernas as the white bodies arrive."

"Are we the white bodies, Dad?"

"Today we are. So we have to slap the factor plenty on for the first few days anyway. Nevertheless, it was good of him, wasn't it."

"Yes, it was, wasn't it?" JJ grew a bit inside as his dad talked to him like a grown up.

They found their bit of beach a few minutes' walk along the sand. Plenty of places to kick the ball around, in and out of the water when the sun got too hot. Or just in and out of the water anyway because it was there.

By midday the sun had got too hot for Gran. Not too hot to take her cardigan off – the cardigan was there for protection. She remembered the stories Harry had told her about how powerful the sun was when he was in the army stationed in Cyprus.

"We're going up there," Molly pointed to some sunshades back off the beach a bit. "It's probably a cafe, I think… a taverna."

"OK, we'll follow you up in a bit. What's the name of it? Oh, I've got it – The Apollo."

Molly took out her little tin of Nivea that she'd had for years, peeled back the tin foil and began rubbing it into her arms. "God, it's bloody hot!"

The waiter arrived with tall glasses of orange juice with ice, and saw the little tin of Nivea. "You shouldn't be using that on such delicate skin."

"Oh this is fine. It's the very latest, you know. It's from the UK."

"I'm sure it is. You're obviously a lady of great taste, but I know how strong the sun is here and you really should have oil gently massaged into your delicate skin."

"Oh go on with you!"

"You should look after yourself. The sun here is very strong."

"Oh, we know that! We've got the factor stuff. Show him, Sinead."

"I'm sure you have, but you should also use lavender oil, to start with. Firmly but gently massage it all over your skin and then… how long are you here for?"

"We're here for ten days. We're on holiday, you know."

Sinead arrived, "I think you're on there, Mam."

"Don't be soft," as she gazed towards the waiter walking away. "Get away with you! He's not bad looking though, is he? He could be right, though," she said as she looked at her tin of Nivea, "Though I've never heard of lavender oil. Anyway, look at that one over there – he can't take his eyes off you!"

"No. Not interested, Mam. Terry's my fellah."

"You're missing him, aren't you love?"

"I love him Mam," tears filling her eyes. "I'm missing him so much."

"I know love. Ten days is not that long, and it will do him no harm at all."

JJ was sitting on the step that led down to the beach, watching fascinated as a barefoot Greek lad meticulously prepared his fishing rod.

Jimmy and Billy arrived and they started looking at the menu for lunch.

"Well, Molly, this is all Greek to me," said Jimmmy.

"That's the main menu. Here's the snacks."

"I knew that. What's an aubergine?" he whispered to Sinead.

"A vegetable."

"I bet you lot didn't know an aubergine was a vegetable."

"Is it, Dad?" JJ was the only one listening.

* * *

They had cheese and ham toasties. When they'd finished, Billy tapped Jimmy with his foot and nodded towards the bar. The two girls from the airport were sitting at the bar.

Jimmy stretched, "Me and Billy are going to have a pint over there."

"Can I go and watch that boy fishing?"

"No, JJ! It's too far... Oh, OK, You keep an eye on JJ, will you, Jimmy." Molly knew she was wasting her breath, but at least it devolved her of some of the responsibility.

* * *

"Hi girls. Didn't we see you on the plane coming over here yesterday?"

"Maybe."

"Oh well, that's great. Are you staying here?"

"Yes, we are."

"Brilliant! So am I. Me and my mate Billy over there. Funny, I didn't see you get off the coach, you know, when it stopped by here yesterday."

"We didn't. We were supposed to be in the hotel down the road, but there was a bit of a mix-up. Anyway, they've put us here."

"Well, I reckon this is your lucky day."

"You reckon?"

"Yeah, great place, great bar, right on the edge of the beach. And then of course there's me, and my mate Billy over there."

"Wasn't that your wife I saw you with yesterday?"

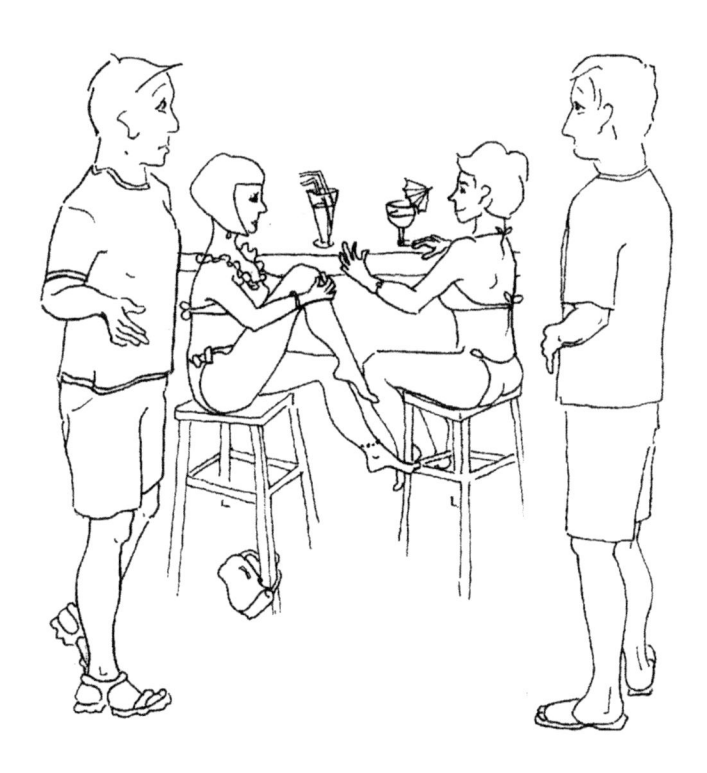

"No, no. She acted a bit like that, didn't she? No, we just met on the plane. Funny woman."

"You're not married, then?"

"Well, slightly, but we've got a very open marriage. She's 'opin' I'll find someone else and piss off – and I'm 'open' for anything."

Billy came over.

"But Billy here's not married, not married at all, are you Billy? Not got a girlfriend neither, have you, mate?"

"Alright, alright, Jimmy! Take it easy. Go and get the drinks."

"Right, two pints… what are you having, girls?"

"We're alright, thank you."

"Oh, come on!"

"No, honestly."

Billy gave him a look.

"OK, OK, two pints."

"Take no notice of him," said Billy, as Jimmy disappeared to the bar.

"Is he your brother or something?"

"No, just mates. He's a good lad, but he has this mission to see me settled down."

Jimmy came back with the drinks. "Here you go, Billy."

Gran came into the bar to escape the sun and sat down nearby. She smiled sweetly, which is a bad sign, and the evidence of her stomach problem drifted over. The girls picked up their drinks and went to sit at a table, as JJ ran over.

"Can I get a fishing rod, Dad?"

"No, we're only here for a few days."

"Ah, go on! I've been watching that lad. Look over there." He tugged Jimmy's arm to get his attention. "Look, Dad, he's over there, he's gone by the rocks now. Can I, Dad? Can I? He's caught three fish. I've seen them. They're this big."

"No, I've told you. No. Look, you haven't had a go at your lilo yet."

"Oh, yeah, the lilo." JJ had forgotten about the lilo. "Let's go and have a go at the lilo, then, Dad."

"Well, hang on a minute! Just let me finish me pint."

Two pints and fourteen reminders about the lilo later, he shouted to Molly, "We're going down to the beach with the lilo. Are you coming?"

"No, we'll stop up here."

"Why don't you go with them, Sinead? I'll wait here with Gran." Gran gave a half-nod in approval.

After a while, the boys were lying back on the sand talking about football. JJ was trying to climb on the lilo in the water. Molly was sunbathing. A freak gust of wind lifted the lilo in the air with JJ hanging on to it.

"Look at me!" he screamed.

"Jesus, Jimmy! Look at him!"

JJ was about eighteen inches off the water, howling with delight.

Jimmy and Billy dashed into the water.

Molly screamed at JJ as the lilo started to gain height, "Let go of the lilo, JJ! Let go of the bloody thing!"

"It's alright, Mam. It's great!"

"Let go of it, JJ, or I'll bloody kill yer!"

Jimmy and Billy were now swimming directly under JJ.

"Now JJ, let go! Do you hear?"

JJ let go of the lilo and dropped. Jimmy tried to catch him and nearly got knocked out in the process. Billy had to drag both of them back to the shore, and the lilo carried off into the sky and disappeared.

Molly grabbed hold of JJ and wrapped a towel round him, then laid into Jimmy.

"You were supposed to be looking after him, you useless get!"

"He's alright!"

"No thanks to you!" Molly pointed to the skyline, "He could have been in Africa for all the notice you were taking!"

"We got him, didn't we? And he's alright. So there's no problem, is there?"

"Where's me lilo gone, Dad? I want another go."

"Billy did, you mean! You, you big lump! Swimming right under him when he lets go of the lilo! Somebody could have got hurt!"

"Like me, you mean?"

Jimmy turned to Billy. "Get no bloody sympathy round here! D'you fancy a pint? Let's go and try that bar over there."

Jimmy and Billy got up and walked towards the bar.

"What's happened to me lilo, Mam?"

Molly shouted, so Jimmy would hear. "Yer Dad'll get you a new one. The useless get! That's the least he can do."

"It wasn't Dad's fault, Mam, it was just the wind."

"No, it never is… it's just that stupid things tend to happen when he's around."

JJ wanted to follow his Dad, but he thought he'd better not and began digging in the sand.

Molly felt a bit guilty for shouting, "How about we go to that taverna to eat tonight, you know, where you had your coffee this morning. Do they do meals?"

"Yeah, I think so. Yeah, let's go there."

"What's it called?"

"I don't know, but I know where it is. Can I go and tell Dad?"

"Yes, OK. Well, see what he says. He might want to go somewhere else."

JJ was already off. He hated it when they had any kind of row, though he always saw his dad's side.

Chapter 6

In the taverna that evening, "Right, moussaka for me, because I'm reliably informed it's got aubergines in it, and that's where we get our genes from, and without your genes you're nothing."

"We get our jeans from the market, Dad, or from the catalogue, don't we, Mam? Not from mascara."

"These are different genes. These are the genes that make up who we actually are."

"Well how come we're who we are, without having that – whatever it was called – before now?"

"Ah well. You're supplied with a certain amount of genes when you're born. But then after that…"

JJ saw the boy who had been fishing now cleaning his rod. "Oh, can I go and watch him, Mam? That was the boy who was fishing."

"OK, but don't go out of the restaurant. What are you going to have to eat?" she shouted after him.

"Chips!" he shouted back.

"You can't just have chips!"

"Chips and sausage… and beans," as an afterthought.

Molly looked at the menu to see if there was anything that looked remotely like sausage.

"Hey look at this! They've got it!" Billy passed the menu to Molly. "Look!"

"Well, bloody hell! Chips, sausage and beans. I'm going to have the moussaka as well – I'm not having him having more genes than me. What are you having, Sinead?"

"Well, I was going to have the moussaka as well, but we can't all have the same thing, so I'll have the souvlaki, with salad."

"And I'll have the pork with the pepper sauce," said Billy, "with tomatoes – you've got to have tomatoes when you're in Greece."

"How about you, Mam? What d'you fancy?"

Gran pointed at the sausage and chips.

"Alright, OK, the same as JJ. You don't fancy the moussaka?"

Gran shook her head. She seldom changed her mind.

"Right, two sausage and chips, two moussakas…" Jimmy gave the order to the waiter, "and wine. Let's get a bottle of white. And you can have half a glass with some lemonade in if you want, Sinead."

"I don't want lemonade in it – I'm not a kid!"

"OK, one glass, then."

Molly looked at Jimmy, "God, we *are* on holiday!"

The food arrived and Molly shouted to JJ. He came running back, "Hey Dad, guess what! His name's Janni, and guess what his dad's name's Janni, and his dad owns this restaurant."

"Well, how about that! What do you know?"

"That's probably the same as calling him Jimmy, you know, JJ."

"Is it, Billy?"

"Well probably. It's either going to be Jimmy or Johnnie, isn't it."

"Cool! I bet it's Jimmy! Aw, that's dead cool, that, isn't it!"

That evening, Jimmy and Billy sat outside Niko's with a beer watching the sunset. An old man walked by leading his donkey, with a little brown dog trotting behind. He touched his hat and smiled as he passed. They smiled back.

Jimmy watched him disappear up the track. "I saw him earlier on. I wonder where he goes?"

* * *

Sinead was the first to wake in the morning. "It's nearly quarter to eight, Dad. We've got to splash the pool."

"Oh, right. OK. Be right there."

Their coffee place was already open. Janni was setting out the tables as they passed. "I'll get the Greek coffee ready for you."

"No, no," shouted Jimmy, laughing.

There were already a few people in the sea. "Ah, we're not the first. Not to worry – we'll splash the pool tomorrow."

They stopped for their coffee on the way back – normal coffee this time. JJ saw his new mate, Janni, walk by and he was reminded about the fishing.

"Can I get a fishing rod, Dad… please?" The please was added as a slight afterthought as if he already knew the answer.

"No, Jimmy. I've already told you. Anyway, we're going to get you a new lilo today. Your mum's seen them in the shop. So after breakfast that's what we're going to do. That's good, isn't it?"

"Yeah… Thanks Dad," but inside he was thinking a lilo *and* a fishing rod would be better.

* * *

Later that morning, Molly was peeling back the foil on her tin of Nivea. Gran was sitting under a parasol and Sinead was sunbathing. The boys were in the water trying to climb on the new lilo and knock whoever was on it off.

The waiter walked towards Molly, who quickly put the Nivea away. He put a small bottle on the table next to Molly. "I'll come back later and put some on your shoulders. The sun is very hot today. What is your name, by the way?"

"Molly, and this is my mother, and this is my daughter, Sinead. She's sixteen, aren't you love," emphasising the mother and daughter bit.

"Ah. Three beautiful ladies… my lucky day. My name is Stavros. I will see you later."

Gran and Sinead looked at each other, and then at Molly.

"What? He's just being friendly, that's all." She looked towards Jimmy in the water and whispered, "Bloody Hell!" under her breath. Molly picked up the bottle and took the top off. "Oh, it does smell nice, though."

Sinead looked at it. "It's probably his own concoction. It's probably an aphrodisiac."

"Oh, don't be soft! Anyway, what d'you mean 'aphrodisiac'? What d'you know about that stuff?" She passed it to her mother, who just looked back expressionless.

Sinead picked the bottle up. "It does smell lovely. It's probably made by his grandmother. His family have probably been making it for generations, high in the hills outside Athens where he was born."

"Yes, well I'm sure you're right, but before he comes back and tells me all that and wants to get touchy feely, I think we should go and find the boys and go for a walk. How about over that way? You see over there. I noticed that yesterday. There's still a bit of shade from the trees by there."

As they wandered through the trees they were surprised to find a small taverna they didn't expect, surrounded by olive trees. They were embracing the whole Corfu experience, apart from the goat's cheese Jimmy ordered, which ranked alongside the Greek coffee of the previous morning. But still, he persevered all the way through, cringing every time he took a bite, with Sinead cringing in sympathy, even mopping up the olive oil and oregano with his bread to leave his plate clean.

Two or three hornets were flying around, which scared the life out of Sinead – and everybody else if the truth were known. Even the local lads were wary, which didn't help.

They were all quite content sitting in the taverna, which they now had to themselves, amongst the dappled shade of the trees. The hornets had buzzed off to pastures new. Billy had nodded off. Gran pretended to, but had just drifted back to the Mississippi. Sinead was reading her book. Molly shifted her chair so she could pick up the sun's rays through the trees. JJ was looking at the menu.

"Oh, look, Dad – they've got them orbingeens."

"Oh, right." Jimmy got up and wandered round, looking at the wild flowers. JJ followed.

"Have they got geens in them, Dad?"

"Oh yes, lad. I expect they have… I expect they have," wondering how long this was going to go on.

They went back and sat down.

"The Greeks eat a lot of aubergines, you know. That's where 'genius' comes from."

Sinead stopped reading her book, but didn't look up.

"The Greeks have had many geniuses in the past, you know. Aristotle, Socrates…"

Sinead looked at him, wondering where he got all this from.

"…Plato," he carried on. "In fact Plato wasn't his real name, you know. His real name was Janni."

"Janni? That's my friend's name, Janni, isn't it, Dad."

"That's right, son. Janni the Greek. When he was a kid he used to ask his mother for a big plate of aubergines, and that's why everybody started calling him Plato."

Sinead turned back to her book, secure in the knowledge that her father was still an idiot.

* * *

They got back to the beach in the late afternoon when the sun was not so fierce. JJ played with his new lilo. Jimmy and Billy talked about football, which was about as intense as a conversation can get.

Molly shouted, "Jesus, Jimmy! The little get's trying to do it again!"

Jimmy looked up and sighed, annoyed at his conversation being interrupted. JJ was running up and down the beach holding his new lilo behind his back, jumping, trying to get airborne.

"Hey, JJ! Don't do that, lad," Jimmy shouted.

"Well, that's not going to stop him!"

"Nothing's going to happen. He's just playing. Leave him alone. That was a freak yesterday – it couldn't happen twice."

"Yeah, famous last words. Do something – it was your idea to bring the lilo."

"I don't remember that?"

But it was obvious Molly wasn't going to let up.

"Oh, for Christ's sake! Pass me bag, Billy." Jimmy fumbled through his bag and took out an air pistol, pointed it at the lilo, shot it, and put the gun back in his bag.

JJ was a bit shocked for a moment as he realised he was trying to run with a limp piece of plastic. Everybody was shocked, stunned into silence, except Jimmy who carried on talking football. "I tell you that formation they tried at the end of last season just won't work, and they'd better…"

But he was interrupted, first by JJ who ran over, "Brilliant, Dad! Give us a go!" then Molly, "Jesus Christ, Jimmy! What d'you think you're doing?"

"I've stopped the lilo, haven't I?"

"You could have killed him, you stupid get!"

"I may not be the best shot in the world, but I can hit a bloody lilo!"

JJ grabbed Jimmy's arm and pointed to a lilo on the sea with a girl floating on it.

"See if you can get that one, Dad. Go ahead, shoot that one. Or give us a go – I bet I can."

"What the hell did you bring that for, Jimmy, you stupid get! And why the hell didn't you have it yesterday?"

"Hang on a minute, I'm getting mixed messages here. Just calm down, there's no harm done."

Billy, Gran and Sinead were watching the shouting bounce backwards and forwards like a tennis match.

But Molly wasn't for calming down. An hour later she was still going at it. She'd gone through the ramifications of handing the gun in to the police, and decided against it as she realised the inevitability of being deported, passports confiscated, the Embassy would be involved, and the newspapers. Probably on the News at Ten back home. For a while she thought about burying it, but a dog might dig it up, or a child.

Billy had gone to the bar and was talking to the two girls from the airport. Gran and the kids were sitting on the steps watching, licking ice creams. JJ had a handkerchief tied round his head, bandit-style, to cover his nose because of Gran's little problem. He lifted the flap up every time he wanted a lick of his ice cream.

The beach was practically deserted, apart from Jimmy getting an ear-bashing from Molly.

Jimmy looked up to the heavens with a plaintive cry, "Please, God, will you shut her up." High up in the sky, a speck appeared, the speck getting bigger and bigger as it got nearer and nearer the ground; what was now beginning to look very much like a lilo was heading to earth. Molly's voice became quieter and quieter, being replaced by The Beatles' song *Maxwell's Silver Hammer*. Then with a huge Kerplop! the lilo returned to the earth and flattened Molly face down in the sand. Jimmy stared up into the sky from where it had come, then turned and walked off the beach leaving Molly face down in the sand with a lilo on her back. He passed the three sitting on the steps, who were staring out towards the lilo and Molly. JJ was trying to lick his ice cream without lifting the flap.

Without looking at them, Jimmy muttered, "You'd better go and get your lilo, and," as an afterthought, "your mother. She's having a lie down."

Chapter 7

Jimmy carried on straight up the steps to the bar without glancing back. "Hello girls. Get us a pint, Billy."

His pint went down in one without touching the sides.

Nobody mentioned the air pistol again. It was as though it had never happened. It was just too bizarre to register. Nobody, that is, except Billy.

"OK, Jimmy, what's the story?"

"What story?"

"The bloody gun story, that's what!"

"It's not a gun, it's an air pistol. Oh look, there's that old geezer with the donkey again."

The old man touched his hat and nodded. They smiled back.

"You were getting on well with the girls, weren't you? Who'd have thought somebody called Gabrielle would come from Rochdale? It's more, well, posh isn't it? I mean *Gabrielle… Rochdale*. Jenny's alright – Jenny could come from Rochdale."

"Don't change the subject. The gun."

"It was Harry's, he gave me it a couple of years ago when he knew his card was marked. He didn't want Daisy getting hold of it. He said she'd finish up killing somebody."

"Oh, and he thought you were safe, did he? I must admit, it was pretty impressive. You just shot the fucking thing and carried on talking without pausing for breath."

43

"Well, it was the football, wasn't it – they've got to get back on top again this year."

"Yeah, yeah – stick with the gun. Why the hell did you bring it?"

"I don't know. I don't know, but I've had this feeling something was going to happen on this holiday."

"Well you shot a lilo."

"I know! It was bloody good that, wasn't it! I was impressed myself. Molly went ape."

"I know! I was there."

"And then the lilo came out of the sky and flattened her."

"It didn't flatten her."

"It bloody did!"

"No, it didn't, it just landed nearby."

"It took her out, I tell you! You weren't there. You were at the bar trying to get your leg over."

"I was just chatting, for Christ's sake! They're nice girls."

"Yeah, right! Anyway, I left her there with the lad's lilo on her back."

"It wasn't Jimmy's lilo – we put that in the bin."

"No, I don't mean that one. I mean yesterday's one – the one that went airborne. That's the one that came down today and twatted her. Well it didn't exactly twat her, it really more just pushed her over and gently pinned her there while I got away."

They both started laughing uncontrollably. Eventually, Billy said, "It couldn't have been JJ's lilo. Lilos blow away all the time."

"Yeah, you're probably right."

"But you still haven't told me why you brought the gun."

"It's them Osama Bin Ladens, isn't? They're all over the place."

"You what?"

"It's them terrorists – you see them on the news every night – they're everywhere."

"What are you talking about, Jimmy? Here, in Corfu? Behave yourself!"

"Could be, Billy. Could be. You never know."

"Osama Bin Laden's not going to be in Corfu!"

"He could be. He could be in Corfu."

"What's Osama Bin Laden going to be doing in Corfu?"

"Having a break, the same as us – a bit of a holiday."

"Ah, piss off!"

"Why not? It's a very stressful job, you know, terrorism."

JJ came running up and stopped the conversation. "I've just seen Janni, Dad. He says he's got a fishing rod he'll lend me. So can I go fishing with him tomorrow?"

"Well, we'll see."

"Thanks, Dad," and ran off.

"Mam! Dad said it's OK!"

"Look, just listen to him! And we wonder how wars start!"

* * *

They had their meal at Niko's that night, having had enough excitement for one day. By ten o'clock the kids and Gran had gone to bed, and Billy went down to the Apollo. Jimmy and Molly shared a bottle of wine outside Niko's, watching the sun go down.

"Seems like we've been here for a month, doesn't it, Moll."

"Yes, it's a beautiful place."

All the hassles of the day drifted away.

"Have you seen that old guy with the donkey and the dog? He's a good old guy. It's funny – have you ever noticed – you take to some people immediately. People you've never met before, as if they're stepping stones in life, just to let you know you're more or less on the right path."

Molly looked long and hard at Jimmy. "You're getting very philosophical in your old age."

Jimmy went inside and up to their room to go to the toilet. JJ called from the bedroom.

"What is it, lad?"

"It was my lilo, Dad. You know, that came back down? It was mine."

"Nah, it could have been anyone's, lad. It often happens, apparently, lilos getting blown about."

"It was mine, Dad. I know!"

"How, son?"

"You're going to give me a crack."

"No I'm not, son. No I'm not."

JJ hesitated. "It was Danny Pritchard at school." He hesitated again, "He told me you can't burn plastic and I didn't believe him, so I…"

"It's alright, lad."

"I got a stick from the fire when no-one was looking, and burnt it on the corner, but it didn't burn, it just crinkled… You're going to give me a crack, aren't you?"

"No, lad, no more cracks."

"And the crinkle was still there. I had a look at it when we brought it back."

"Yes, I know, lad."

"How do you know? Did you see it?"

"No, Jim – because you told me it was. Now, it's time to go to sleep. Remember, fishing tomorrow. Big day, hey?"

"Yes, Dad." He curled up into a ball. "Goodnight, Dad."

"Goodnight, son."

"It's our secret, isn't it, Dad?"

"What is?"

* * *

No early morning swim. They'd overslept. Jimmy and Billy were sitting outside Niko's with a pot of tea, when the old man appeared, strolling up the track with donkey and dog.

"Morgen," he said, as he passed.

"Morgen," the boys replied, instinctively.

"He thinks we're German," said Billy.

"Must do. Don't look German, do we?"

"Must do to him. The Greeks had a lousy war, didn't they, especially the islands. I read a book about it. I think it was Crete. The partisans used to come down from the mountains and attack the German positions then disappear back into the mountains. The Germans would never find them, so they took reprisals out on the villagers."

"Man's inhumanity. It's all forgotten now... well, not forgotten, but forgiven."

The conversation stopped suddenly as Gran appeared walking up the track, her hair wet lying down her back instead of the normal way tied up in a bun, her cardigan over her arm.

"Splashed the pool," she said, as she sat down and put her bag on the floor. "Get us a cup of tea."

* * *

JJ watched Janni meticulously preparing his fishing rod. He took a tin out of his bag and showed JJ. The box had two compartments; one full of little wriggling worms, and the other bits of bread.

"Sometimes the worms are better, and sometimes the bread."

"Where did you get the worms?"

"You have to go to the beach early in the morning as the tide goes out and dig in the sand."

"D'you have to do that every day?"

"Sometimes."

"If you go tomorrow, can I come with you?"

"Well, you'll have to ask your dad. This morning it was about six o'clock."

"Oh."

"How old are you?"

"Nine, nearly ten. How old are you?"

"Thirteen. You have to go then or the worms are gone. This is your rod. It's not as good as this one, but it's still good. It's the one I had when I was about your age. It only takes about twenty minutes to get the worms, then I go and help my dad in the taverna."

"Aren't you helping your dad today?"

"I have been, but he let me finish a bit early so we could go fishing."

"Did he?" JJ felt a bit special. "None of my mates go fishing."

All the time they were talking, Janni was preparing his rod. He showed JJ the hook. "This bit is very sharp, and this bit stops the hook coming out when the fish bites it." He took a worm, very carefully put the hook through it, and cast the line. The line went far out into a pool between the rocks.

JJ watched, fascinated, as the float bobbed up and down in the sea.

"Can I do mine now?"

"In a minute. It takes a bit of practice to get it in the pool. Perhaps we should go over there." He pointed to a slightly easier place.

"No, let's stay here. I can practice."

The float suddenly started bobbing faster, and Janni started wrestling with his rod, and reeled in a fish about six inches long. He very carefully unhooked the fish and gently let it go back into the water.

JJ stared in disbelief.

"Too small."

"Too small," JJ whispered to himself.

Jimmy left the others at the Apollo and wandered over.

"How's it going, lads?"

"Oh, it's great, Dad. We've caught one fish, Dad, but it was a bit small so we let it go back, didn't we, Janni. This is my rod. It was Janni's when he was about the same age as me. Wasn't it, Janni? You cast it into that pool there. That means…" JJ went through the motions of how to cast, without actually doing it. "Because that's where the fish are, isn't it, Janni. I'll be doing it proper in a minute, but it takes a lot of practice, doesn't it, Janni."

Janni nodded.

"Right, well I'd better leave you two fishermen to practice then."

* * *

"Is he alright?" asked Molly.

"Yeah, he's having a whale of a time – providing he doesn't catch a whale."

"Has he caught anything?"

"No. He hasn't started yet. Janni's showing him the ropes. He's fine. Fancy a walk, Billy? Fancy going up the road to that one over there? What is it – oh, there we are – the Acropolypse."

"Yeah, OK."

"Acropolis." Sinead corrected him without opening her eyes.

As the boys were walking towards the bar, Gabrielle and Jenny were walking towards them.

"Watch this, Billy boy," Jimmy got ready to swing into action.

As the girls approached they smiled at Billy. Gabrielle, hands by her side, twiddled her fingers at Billy and he reciprocated. They passed by.

"What the bloody hell was that?"

"What the bloody hell was what?"

Jimmy repeated the twiddle, exaggerating it. "This business – that's what."

"Oh, it's nothing."

"That's not nothing. When did you become all pally?"

"Last night while you and Molly stopped at Niko's I had a couple of drinks with Jenny and Gabbie."

"Oh, Gabbie, is it! You sly dog. Did you give her one?"

"No, I didn't!" said Billy, a bit indignant.

They arrived at the bar.

"Hello, Billy – a beer?" asked the waiter.

"Yes, please."

"Same as last night?"

"Yes, two please," looking at Jimmy for approval.

Jimmy was stunned.

"Nice place, this, isn't it," Billy was looking at the menu, "This looks good… shall we come here for our tea?"

Jimmy felt a bit dejected and redundant: JJ was off fishing with his mate, Gran had splashed the pool, Billy had his girlfriends – and now he knows all the waiters.

"Yeah, why not? Seems like a nice place. Let's have a look at the menu."

* * *

Back at the Apollo, Stavros arrived and handed Molly another little bottle.

"This is primrose oil," he said, "This is also very good."

"Er, er.. I noticed, there's no label on it."

"Ah, that's because it's made by my family. My grandmother makes it. My family has done this for generations."

"Oh, that's nice. Where's your family from?"

"Just outside Athens. A small village high up in the hills."

Molly and Sinead looked at each other.

"Anyway, this oil is also very good, but it needs to be massaged all over your body, then by the end of the week oil of roses."

"Who d'you think you are – Zorba the Greek?"

"Ah, you know Zorba? Zorba's dance? I am also a good dancer, you know."

"Yes, in your head!"

"Perhaps I will show you how to dance the Greek way before the end of your holiday. Anyway, I will get some more oil for you, then the English Rose will become a Greek Goddess, glistening with a Greek tan and even more beautiful than you are now."

Molly was not sure how to handle all this attention. "I think you're a bit horny."

"Horny? What is horny?"

"Hornet. Hornet! You know, wasps. Bumble Bee!" Molly swatted an imaginary wasp in the air. "They're all over the place, aren't they?"

Stavros looked a bit confused, and went to clear some empty glasses. Molly watched him as he walked away and thought, *I'm feeling a bit Bumble Bee meself, now. Bloody hell.*

Chapter 8

JJ stayed fishing all day, apart from fifteen minutes when Molly dragged him back for a sandwich. Twice JJ cast into the pool, but mostly it landed in the rocks and Janni had to climb down to free it. No fish – but it was the best day ever. Janni caught four. JJ couldn't have been more proud if he had caught them himself.

Jimmy and Billy got to the Apollo before the others, and they were sitting down talking footie when a Greek Orthodox priest walked in – long black robe, long beard, tall hat – and started talking to the bar owner. Jimmy saw him and tried to suppress his shock. He put his hand over his mouth and hurriedly whispered.

"Jesus Christ, Billy! He's just walked in."

"Who has?"

"Over there by the kitchen door, it's Osama Bin Laden. Don't look."

Billy turned to look.

"Don't look!"

Billy couldn't resist. "That's not Osama Bin Laden – that's a Greek minister, you soft get!"

"That's bloody Osama Bin Laden, I tell you."

"No he's not. He's an Orthodox priest. He's a priest, Jimmy, from the church."

"They always are, Billy," in muted tones, "They're always

something to do with the church — that's their cover. That's Osama Bin Laden, I tell you."

"Well, if it is, why isn't he wearing a turban? And why's he got a black robe and not a white one? And that fellah's wearing a priest's hat."

"Course he is, you soft get! That's part of his cover. And, in any case, he's on holiday. People wear stupid stuff when they're on holiday. Look at you with that stupid shirt with a seagull on the back."

"It's not a seagull! It's a bird of paradise."

"Exactly! You wouldn't walk around Liverpool wearing that. You'd get arrested."

Jimmy was thinking he was making a bit of progress with his theory. "You see that's why they haven't caught him, Billy. See, they're looking in Afghanistan and Pakistan. All the obvious places. And that's why they haven't caught him. You've Got To Think Outside The Box."

"You don't." Billy took a sidelong look at the priest, "Oh, OK then, well you'd better go and shoot him."

Jimmy paused for a minute. "The gun's in my room. Should I go and get it?"

"In your room? In your room, Jimmy? Clint Eastwood wouldn't forget his gun!"

"I can nip back and get it now. It'll only take me ten minutes."

"No, leave it for now, we'll get him tomorrow."

JJ turned up, breaking the tension, followed by the others.

"Who're you going to get, Dad?"

"No-one. We're getting no-one. We're just trying to get hold of a telly to keep up with the footie." He turned to Billy, "Hush about this. We'll talk about it later. Don't say a word."

As the evening drew on and the merriment took over, Jimmy forgot all about Public Enemy Number One, and became fascinated by Dimitri, the gay waiter. He noticed every time a party had finished their meal, Dimitri went over and offered them a drink. Jimmy knew that any second he was going to do the same to them. He whispered to Billy, "Watch this. He'll come over and ask us if we want to have a drink."

"Have you all enjoyed your meal?" asked Dimitri.

"Yes, very nice, thank you."

"Would you like to have a drink with me?"

"Oh, that's very nice of you. Where would you like to go?"

"I meant would you like…"

"Oh, that's a good idea, Dimitri," said Molly. "Why don't you two run off and have a nice drink?"

Dimitri saw through all of this instantly, "Well, I'll finish here in about an hour, and I do know a bar. We could go there for a nice quiet drink."

"No, no – I mean…" Jimmy was starting to panic, "It was just a joke."

"Oh, go on, Jimmy. You and Dimitri go and have a drink. You could go to that club, what's it called, you know where the – what's the name of it?" She mouthed, "It's where the gays go."

"Can I come with you, Dad?"

"Shurrup, JJ!"

Dimitri looked round at the few remaining diners, "I may not be an hour… For now, can I get you some drinks?"

"Can I have ouzo, Dad?"

"Shurrup," said Sinead.

"Let me get you our house special." Dimitri winked at Billy and went to get the drinks.

* * *

The next morning at the beach, JJ was back at the rocks fishing with Janni. Molly leaned over to Jimmy and whispered, "Me mam's forgotten to take her tablet."

"Oh, shit!"

"Exactly. Will you go and get them, or shall we all go back?"

Jimmy thought for a moment, "OK, where are they?"

"They're on the sideboard thing in our bedroom."

"Alright, I'll be back as quick as I can."

It was about a twenty-five minute walk to get back to Niko's from the far end of the beach which had become their special place. Jimmy collected the tablets and was just about to start back to the beach, when the old man appeared, complete with donkey and dog, and beckoned Jimmy to follow him. Jimmy looked at his watch and pointed towards the beach, but the old man insisted. Jimmy followed him, with donkey and dog, wondering where the hell he was going. They wandered up the track in the opposite direction, and then along a narrower track, through a broken gate. There were rows and rows of vegetables.

"Salad," the old man said, and beckoned Jimmy to follow. He walked carefully between the rows, pausing every now and then to bend down and pick some and hand them to Jimmy, saying, "Salad," as he pushed them into Jimmy's hand. Spring onions, lettuce, and stuff Jimmy didn't know. Then to a broken-down shed at the end. He went in and sorted through the tomatoes to find the ripest and handed Jimmy four. "Salad."

"Thank you, thank you very much," Jimmy was quite moved. He couldn't shake the old man's hand because of all the salad.

"Salad," the old man said again, and nodded.

Jimmy made his way back to Niko's. He put the salad in his room. He had no idea how long the detour had taken, and started walking quickly back to the beach. Then he saw the old man, complete with donkey and dog, walking towards him.

How the hell did he get there? It was definitely the same old guy, complete with dog and donkey.

As they met, the old guy nodded and smiled in the usual way, and pointed to a narrow track on the left. He gestured to Jimmy to go down there. Jimmy pointed to his watch and mouthed, "I'm in a bit of a rush. Got to get back to the beach."

The old man nodded and pointed down the track again. Jimmy had no choice. He began walking down the narrow track. He stopped and turned to see if the old man was following, but he wasn't – he was just standing at the end, and signalled to keep walking.

Where the hell am I going? he thought as he carried on. A small white cottage appeared on the right, with a buxom lady bringing in her washing. She smiled when she saw Jimmy and pointed to a footpath at the side of the cottage and gestured to Jimmy to go down there.

"I'm looking for the beach," said Jimmy, a bit louder than he needed. She smiled. *She's not understanding a word.*

She just smiled and pointed down the footpath again. About twenty or thirty yards down the path – difficult to say – he stepped on to the beach, right at the part where his family were.

"Oh, you weren't long – have you got her pills?"

Jimmy wasn't quite sure where to start. "I found a short cut."

"Oh, good. Well, give us the tablets."

Jimmy looked back for the path. He couldn't see it. *Must be further along.*

"There's a path over there somewhere."

"Right, well show us later. Billy's down on the rocks with the boys."

Jimmy decided to go and find the boys, but took a detour so as to make sure he knew where the path was for later so he could show everybody how clever he'd been, but he couldn't find it. It wasn't there. It had to be there. But it wasn't – it was all different. He thought he was looking in the right place, but it just wasn't there.

"Look at these, Dad! Janni's caught three fish. Look at that one – it's really big. I haven't caught one yet, but I'm getting dead good at the casting. Aren't I, Janni! Look at this. Stand back, Dad." Jimmy cast out and it landed on the rocks. "Ah, it doesn't do that all the time."

Billy climbed down to free it.

JJ tried three more times, without success. "I'll get it next time. I bet you!"

"Yeah, well it does take practice, lad. But it's nearly lunchtime now. Why don't we go and get something to eat and you can try again later on."

"Ah, just one more go, hey? Just one more go?"

"Well, OK."

But JJ missed.

"You can't do fishing on an empty stomach, in any case – you've got to be relaxed when you're fishing – it's no good trying too hard. Isn't that right, Janni?"

"Yes, the fish won't come if you try to rush them."

Jimmy didn't mention the short cut any more, but he kept looking for it. It had to be there somewhere. Didn't it? He didn't mention the salad, either, just in case it wasn't there when he got back. But it was.

"What's all this?" said Billy when he saw the salad on the table.

"Salad from the old geezer. The old guy with the donkey gave us it. Good of him, wasn't it."

He wondered about showing Billy the old guy's allotment, but he was scared it wouldn't be there, either.

"What are you going to do with all this?" said Billy.

"Make a sideboard... It's salad, you idiot! You eat it – you get some bread or ham. Or if the old guy comes back we can shoot the donkey and cook it."

"That's going to be a bit tough."

"It'll be a bit tough on the old fellah."

"Are you serious about Osama Bin Laden?"

"Too right. It's definitely him. We'll talk about it later, but we've got to be quick and make a plan. We've only got a few days left."

"Well, we could tell the cops – or phone the FBI or the CIA. Which one does terrorists? It'll be the CIA won't it."

"You've got to take this seriously, Billy. Anyway, they wouldn't believe you. And anyway, we found him. Imagine the glory – we'd be heroes for life. I've been working on a plan. Shush!" he said as Gran and Sinead appeared, and quickly changed the subject. "So Gerrard's going to be absolutely brilliant this season…"

Gran gave Jimmy a long look. "You weren't talking about football."

* * *

Later that afternoon, Jimmy and Billy hid behind the wall of the Acropolis to see if Osama Bin Laden came there at the same time as he had done yesterday. Sure enough, he did.

"There you go. What did I tell you? Terrorists are creatures of habit. That's what lets them down – they become too confident."

"Where the hell did you get all that from?"

"It was on the back of the cornflakes. Tomorrow, Molly and the girls are going to the market, which means they'll be out for a couple of hours at least. I'll get them to take JJ."

* * *

The next morning Molly, seeing Jimmy and Billy whispering, said, "What are you two plotting?"

"Nothing."

"Well, we're off to the market. We'll be back about twelve. What are you two going to be doing?"

"Well, I thought we might go and capture Osama Bin Laden."

"OK, well don't make a mess. I've tidied up."

Jimmy and Billy looked at each other. Jimmy whispered, "See what I mean? Nobody believes."

As soon as the coast was clear they met up in Jimmy's bedroom.

"OK, Clint. What's the plan?"

Jimmy put a melon on the pillow. "Just time me. I reckon I've got to re-load and fire in less than five seconds."

"You're going to shoot him?"

"Well, slightly."

"Slightly? You can't go around killing people!"

"I'm not going to kill him. It's a bloody air pistol. You can't kill anybody with an air pistol."

"Well, if you're not going to kill him, what are you going to do?"

"It'll give him a bloody headache, won't it. He'll want to sit down for a bit, and that's when we grab him. Look – we've got to practice. We've only got two hours."

Billy sighed. He wasn't really sure about this.

"OK. This is the dummy run." He positioned the melon on the pillow again. Gun in hand, he opened his tin of pellets. "OK, Billy, tell me when to go."

Billy stared at his watch, and stared at his watch.

"Are you going to tell me when to go?"

"I'm waiting for the second finger to get round to the twelve."

"You don't have to wait for it to get round to the twelve. You can go on fifteen or thirty or something."

"Go!" shouted Billy.

"I'm not ready now!" Jimmy screamed. "Right, let's do it again. I've had a few goes – see?" He showed Billy the melon with three tiny holes in it.

Billy cringed. "OK, let's do it."

"OK, well, we'll try a dummy run first."

"OK... Go!"

Jimmy swung into action. He broke the barrel and pretended to put the pellet in, snapped the barrel shut, pointed at the melon and pretended to fire. "Right. How long?"

"Have you fired?"

"Yes I've fucking fired!"

"Well you should have said bang then, or something. When we were kids and you used to fire the gun you always used to make a Kapow!! sound, didn't you."

"We're just wasting time here. Right, I'll put a real pellet in it this time. You'll hear the crack – and that means I've fired it. OK?"

"OK, right. But it's no good getting rattled. You're not going to be able to shoot straight if you're all wound up."

"I... fucking... know... that," said Jimmy very slowly and deliberately. "OK, let's get it right this time."

"OK. Ready... Go!"

Jimmy broke the barrel, put the pellet in, closed the barrel, aimed... Crack! "How long?"

"You missed the melon."

"How long?"

"Six seconds. But you missed the melon."

"Six seconds, eh? That's pretty good."

"I hate to be repeating myself, Jimmy, but you missed the fucking melon."

"A detail, Billy, that's all."

"A pretty important one. Look, concentrate on getting your accuracy and build the speed up from there." *I can't believe I'm saying this.* "What's the importance of the time for re-loading, because you're going to have one in the gun already, aren't you?"

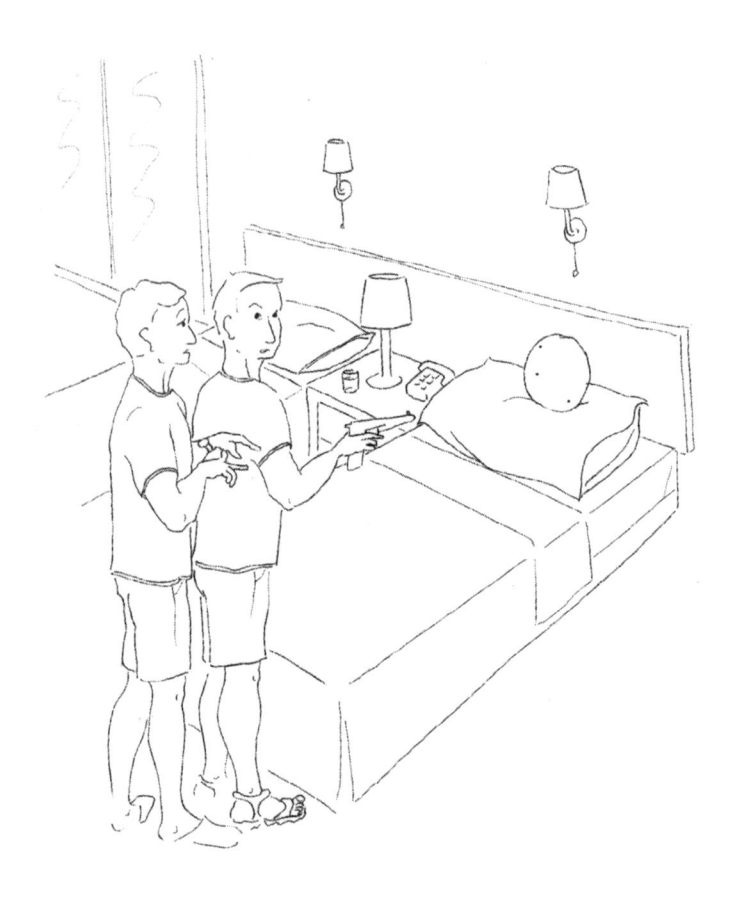

"Well, it's going to take more than one shot to bring him down, isn't it."

"Is it? How many?"

"About five, I reckon."

"Five?" Billy gasped.

"Well it may not take five, but whatever it takes to give him a headache so he wants to sit down for a bit – then we grab him."

"And what's going to make him stay put all the time you're being Buck Rodgers?"

"Ah, well I've thought about that. You're chatting to him, aren't yer. Hold him in conversation."

"What?"

"You know, talk to him about something."

"Oh, right. Like what? Ask him how his family's doing in Iraq?"

"No! Tell him a story, or a joke. Tell him that one about the butcher and the bag of carrots."

"You told me that was a terrible story."

"Yeah, but he doesn't know that."

"You want me to go up to public enemy number one, who I've never met before incidentally, and tell him a not very funny story about a butcher and a bag of carrots while you're taking pot shots at his melon?"

"Yes, that's about it."

"That's a lousy plan."

"OK, then, smart arse. What's yours?"

"I HAVEN'T GOT ONE!"

"OK then. Right. Well, let's calm down… and perfect this one."

"In two hours!"

Jimmy glanced at his watch, "Well, it's about an hour and a half now. Right then, OK. He'll probably go and stand in the same place by the kitchen. You start talking to him. I come out from behind the Coca Cola machine, firing – say four or five seconds each shot. It'll all be over in a minute – less than a minute – half a minute. He'll probably look for a chair to sit down, so we'll have to have one over there. Then you dash over and tie him up."

"I don't need to dash anywhere. I'm standing next to him."

"A very good point, Billy. I hadn't thought of that. Good, you're getting into the swing of it now."

Chapter 9

By the time the others returned the plan was pretty well perfected… ish.

"What's all this stuff in your suitcase?" said Molly.

"Oh, that's salad."

"What, lettuce and tomatoes and – what's this weird stuff? Where did all this come from?"

"The old man gave it to me. You know, the old man with the donkey? Nice old guy."

"He gave you all this stuff, and you thought you'd put it in your suitcase?" She went to the kitchen to get a bowl.

"I thought it would keep it fresh."

"What, with your smelly clothes, in this heat? We could have got some ham and bread and made sandwiches this morning."

"That's exactly what I told Billy."

"I think one of us is losing the plot round here."

* * *

Later, back on the beach, Billy and Jimmy were waist-high in the water, ironing out the fine details.

"I've decided it's only going to take three to bring him down."

"What – three? Why three?"

"On account of I've only got three pellets left. But I tell you what – I've got an idea how we can double-check we've got the right guy. Let's go over by the rocks and pretend we're looking after the kids."

Two small figures were snorkelling by the rocks. JJ and Janni climbed out to dry off. Janni got out a plastic box, opened it and gave JJ a piece of cheese, a tomato and a chunk of bread. JJ looked at it very suspiciously then bit into a piece of bread. In a moment or two they were both tucking into it and laughing at the tourists in the water. They were becoming really good mates. JJ took a bite out of the tomato as if it was an apple, and enjoyed it.

A few minutes later, silhouetted against the skyline, two small figures at the edge of the rocks were finishing their cheese and tomato. Two or three yards higher up the rocks were two bigger silhouettes sitting down, deep in concentration, finalising their daring plan.

Molly looked at Gran, "They're plotting something."

"There's a way we can make sure it's Osama Bin Laden," Jimmy whispered.

"How?"

"Well, what's the first thing he's going to pack when he's going away on holiday?"

"A Kalashnikov?"

"No!" said Jimmy with some exasperation. "You haven't brought your fork-lift truck, have you? No, it's going to have to be the Ambre Solaire, isn't it – he's going to have to slap on the factor plenty."

"Oh, behave yourself. He's not going to be sunbathing."

"Course he is. Everybody comes to Corfu to get the rays on the old bod, and I bet that bod hasn't seen the sunshine in four decades – he's probably white as a sheet."

"But he's not white, is he."

"No, you know what I mean. He'll be pasty-looking, won't he. He'll have this drawn, dark, weather-beaten face with a long black beard – on top of a white skinny body."

"Skinny body? How d'you get that?"

"Well, he's not on the front line, is he? He's not going to look like Arnold Schwarzenegger."

"No, but he might sound like Arnold Schwarzenegger."

"I'll give you that. D'you think he's going to be wearing boxers, or Speedos?"

"I haven't really given it a lot of thought."

"He may not be wearing anything. Some of these fellers wear nothing under the white robe, you know. They've probably got todgers like tree trunks."

"Where the hell did you get all that from – the back of the cornflakes?"

"Probably."

Billy was feeling decidedly uncomfortable. He couldn't get the image out of his head of Osama Bin Laden lying back on a sun bed with a tree trunk swinging around. "I'm not entirely happy with the image you're painting here, Jim."

"No, well neither am I, but you've got to face the gruesome details. You've got to prepare for the unexpected. That's my motto."

"I didn't even know you had a motto."

"Oh yes. So where's he going to be? He's not going to be on the beach, so we can rule that out."

"Can we?"

"Yes, of course. He'd have had enough sand in his flip-flops over the years. And he's not going to be at the Apollo, either, I reckon, or we'd have seen him… I reckon he'll be at the hotel where the girls should have stayed. That's probably why the girls had to move: he's got their room."

* * *

Later on that afternoon, pursuing their search, they arrived at the hotel reception in T-shirts, shorts, sandals and dark glasses, looking like two CIA agents on holiday.

"Can I help you?" said the receptionist.

"We're looking for Osama Bin La…" Jimmy dug Billy in the ribs before he could finish.

"Sam Binliner," said Jimmy quickly, "D'you know if he's staying here?"

"That's an unusual name," said the receptionist.

"Yeah. Yes, we call him that because his missus used to call him a bag of rubbish."

While the confused receptionist was looking through the guest list, they carried on towards the swimming pool.

Despite the distractions of blonde hair and pink tits, there was obviously nobody remotely resembling Public Enemy.

There was a sombre air as they walked back towards Niko's.

Deep down they knew they weren't going to find him sitting on a deckchair puffing on a travel pack of hubble-bubble. They were just looking for some kind of overwhelming evidence to support their outrageous plan. But then they knew if that evidence was there the place would be teaming with cops and army, and gone would be their moment of glory. They stopped at a small taverna they hadn't been to before so they could talk.

"I'm scared, Jimmy."

"Me too."

"What if he has a team of minders, a team of bodyguards? What if six of them come charging out of the woodwork, screaming, swinging..." he paused for a moment. "What would they be swinging?"

"Tree trunks, probably."

They roared laughing, which verged on hysteria, which served to relieve some of the pressure, the tension that was building. When it all subsided, "Shall we do it, Billy?"

"Yeah," he nodded.

"Are you sure?"

He nodded again.

"Are you definitely sure?"

"Don't push it, Jimmy. No, I'm not definitely sure."

"OK then. It's got to be tonight. He gets there about six. We know that. I'll get there about twenty to. I'll be able to see him coming way before, so I can get in position."

Chapter 10

Jimmy walked into the Acropolis bar just after five-thirty, nervously looking around, his hand resting on his bulging bum bag. The bar was empty. He was there early so he would have time for a pint of courage. The waiter poured a large beer as Jimmy watched the football on the television.

"Ah, you like the football," said the waiter. "Who's your team?"

"Liverpool, of course. The best."

"Liverpool are not the team they used to be."

"Ah, they'll be back, mate. Premiership champions next year, I tell you."

Jimmy started to relax now as the conversation had got on to football. For the moment he'd forgotten his mission. Some two hundred yards away the priest was walking in the direction of the Acropolis bar. Quietly in the background was the Beatles' song *Maxwell's Silver Hammer*.

> *...bang bang Maxwell's silver hammer*
> *comes down upon his head.*
> *Maxwell's silver hammer*
> *made sure that he was dead...*

"We destroyed your lot, Olympiacos. Three-one. Brilliant goal by Stevie in the last minute."

"Gerrard is good, if you can keep hold of him."

"Oh, he's staying alright. No doubt about that."

The waiter went to serve someone else.

The priest was getting nearer, and the music of *Maxwell's Silver Hammer* was getting louder. Jimmy looked around him to see where the music was coming from.

Back in school again,
Maxwell plays the fool again.,
Teacher gets annoyed.
Bang, Bang…

The sound of the music disappeared as a thought bubble appeared over his head:

LIVERPOOL 1 – MANCHESTER UNITED 2.

Jimmy scowled, and concentrated with all his might. The thought bubble changed:

LIVERPOOL 2 – MANCHESTER UNITED 1.

Jimmy beamed as the score changed. As the waiter walked past, "…and we'll win the Champions League next year, I tell you."

The priest tapped Jimmy on the shoulder. He turned and jumped out of his skin.

"Oh, I do beg your pardon. I didn't mean to startle you."

Jimmy didn't know what to say.

"I hope I'm not disturbing you. Are you alright?"

"No, I'm just waiting for my mate, Billy boy. He'll be here in a minute."

"Yes, I saw you with your family, last night, was it? And I couldn't help noticing… I hope you don't mind me asking… are you a man of God?"

"Me? No. Yes. I'm a Liverpool supporter."

The priest smiled. "Ah, the famous Liverpool sense of humour. It's just that you have an aura – a glow – as if you are a Chosen One."

"Me – a chosen one?"

"Yes, you have an aura. It's very rare. I've heard about it, though I've never seen it."

Jimmy looked over his left shoulder, then his right, but he couldn't see anything. "That'll be the ouzo," he said. "It's pretty strong stuff, you know. I've had one or two."

The priest laughed. "You're a funny man, Jimmy Downie. That'll help you a lot. No, it's not the alcohol. I think you're a special person. Are you passionate about any particular religion?"

"Liverpool."

The priest smiled and held out his hand. "My name is Father Jakovis."

Jimmy shook his hand.

"Jimmy. Jimmy Downie."

"Yes, I know."

"You know my name?"

"Yes, I do. Perhaps we'll have time to have a talk? I don't expect now is convenient. When do you go back?"

"In a couple of days."

"Well, if you can make time, I would like to talk. I'm usually at the Chapel – you know where it is, do you, at the edge of the square?"

"Yes," said Jimmy, a bit stunned.

Father Jakovis saw Billy walking in, wearing a motorcycle helmet. "Well, I see your friend's arriving now and, er… well, enjoy the rest of your stay, and do try and make it."

Father Jakovis nodded to Billy and left.

"What was all that?" said Billy. "You were very pally with Osama Bin Laden."

"No, he's not, you know. He's actually a priest. He's a very nice man. You've got him all wrong."

"I must stop doing that. Hang on a minute, Jimmy, let's get this straight. I told you he was a priest at the very beginning."

"No, I know. But he's a very nice man, you know. He's with the church, you know."

"Well, you'd never have guessed that. You'd never tell by looking at him."

Jimmy looked at Billy's crash hat. "Where did you park your bike?"

"Just button it, will you."

"No, it's a very nice hat."

Billy scowled at Jimmy and pointed a finger at him. "Just shut it, Jimmy, and get us a pint."

Jimmy ordered a pint. Billy dropped the crash hat on the floor and kicked it under the table. His pint arrived, and they turned to watch the football on the television.

* * *

"None of us fancy much to eat tonight – I don't know about you two," said Molly. "I think we're all a bit knackered. Must be the sun. What do you fancy doing?"

"I feel a bit the same myself. It's been a bit of a funny day."

"You can say that again," whispered Billy.

JJ saw the crash hat under the table. "Whose is that?"

"It's Billy boy's. Show him Billy."

"Ah, great, Billy. Where's your bike?"

"Under the hat. It's only a small one."

JJ put the hat on and started running round the bar as if on a motorbike.

"Let's just go and get a pizza, Mam," said Sinead.

"Yeah, may as well. Get no sense around here. We're going to the pizza place. Are you coming?"

"Yeah, we'll follow on in a bit."

As they left, JJ kicked the hat back under the table. Jimmy and Billy returned to their pints and the football. Jimmy looked in the mirror and reflected on what Father Jakovis had said.

"Can you see anything around me?"

"Can I see anything around you?"

"Yeah, kind of round me. Can you see anything?"

Billy had a good hard look and think. "It's difficult to say."

"I know," said Jimmy, thoughtfully.

"I think you need a drink. D'you fancy an ouzo?"

"No. Better not. I think I might have an early night as well. I think the sun may have got to me a bit."

"I think it must have done. Come on, have another beer."

"Aye, go ahead. I'll have a beer."

* * *

It was about nine-thirty and the lads hadn't got back yet. Molly wasn't surprised. Sinead and Gran were going to have an early night. JJ was already asleep. So Molly decided to walk down and find them, and maybe have a drink. As she got to the Apollo, Billy was just leaving.

"Where's Jimmy?"

"He's crashed out. He's on a sunbed at the front. He's had a couple of pints of Stella."

"Oh, that'll do it. Where are you going?"

"I was just going to wander up to the Acropolis for half an hour. D'you want to come?"

"No thanks. Better go and find him."

She ordered a drink and then went out to the front to find Jimmy, and there he was, stretched out on a sunbed, sleeping like a baby. She tried to wake him, but years of experience told her she was wasting her time. *Best let him sleep it off,* and went back into the bar for her drink.

Molly finished her drink and went to find Billy at the Acropolis. He was talking to Gabbie and Jenny. The Acropolis was busy – it was Greek Night. Zorba's Dance came on, and the men started their performance, including Stavros. He caught Molly's eye and smiled.

75

Chapter 11

The next morning in Niko's,

"But Mam, I want to go fishing with Janni!"

"You've been with Janni all week, and we're going back tomorrow. I want the family to be together. So we're all going on the bus to Corfu Town, and that's that."

"That's why I want to go fishing," muttered JJ under his breath, "Cos it's our last day."

Janni ran up. "I'm sorry, Jimmy, I can't go fishing. I've just got to help my dad a bit today. I promised him and I forgot."

JJ felt a bit better that it wasn't all his fault. "Oh, well that's OK because I've got to go to Corfu Town on the stupid bus, and it's our last day."

"What time do you get back?"

"Mum, what time does the bus get back?"

"Hello, Janni. Er, about five o'clock I think."

"Well, we'll still have a couple of hours – we could still go then if you like."

"Yeah, defo."

Janni put his hand in his pocket, pulled out his pocket knife and handed it to JJ. "You have that."

JJ stared at the knife and put out his hand. Janni put the knife in JJ's hand and ran off. JJ stared after Janni as he disappeared, then looked back at the knife.

Molly shouted, "Come on you lot! The bus'll be here in a minute."

After the bus had been travelling a few minutes, JJ whispered to his Dad, "I want to get Janni a prezzie and I don't know what to get him."

"Oh, don't worry about that, lad. Men don't do stuff like that."

"They do sometimes... I heard you and Mam saying you were going to give Nikolas a decent tip. What's a decent tip, Dad?"

"Well, you've got a point there, but a tip's different from buying somebody a present. That's what girls do."

JJ was dying to show his dad the knife but he was scared he'd take it off him – or worse, make him give it back.

This was the last day, and Jimmy was trying to push the weird stuff out of his mind. He hadn't spent much time with Sinead, not like he wanted, not like he'd intended. He wasn't sure what to talk to a sixteen year old girl about, and there was always JJ or Billy around. But that was just an excuse; he should have made more of an effort. He remembered a couple of days ago Sinead being chatted up by a local Greek lad. Jimmy didn't like the look of him and went over. The lad walked away when he saw Jimmy. He should have made time to have a talk with Sinead then, but he didn't.

JJ had been thinking about his knife for a long time. He took it out of his pocket and showed his dad.

"What's this, lad?" Jimmy took hold of it.

"Janni gave it to me. It was his and he gave it to me."

"Wow, hey! Can I open it?"

JJ hadn't even done that. "OK, be careful."

Jimmy opened the big blade. "This is a bit special."

"It's a bit scratched, and it's got a little bash mark there."

"Oh, you don't worry about stuff like that. That means it's

been used a lot, and loved by the person that gave you it. And you'll remember that every time you look at it."

"That means I can keep it?"

"Well, hang on a moment. Your mam won't like it."

"Do we have to tell her, Dad?"

"Yes, we do. We don't have secrets like that. The best thing... can I look after it for you? And I'll tell your mam when the time's right."

"Are, eh, Dad!"

"Knives can be very dangerous. Can you leave it with me for the moment, while I think what's best? Is that why you wanted to give Janni a prezzie?"

"Yeah, it was really."

"Right, well let's see how I can explain. Janni doesn't expect a present back. He gave you that knowing it would probably be your first knife, and your first knife is something you never forget."

"D'you remember your first knife, Dad?"

"Oh yeah," he lied. "Janni giving you his knife makes you kind of brothers. So you buying something from the shops wouldn't be quite the same, would it? You'd have to give him something like an arm or a foot or something to equal it."

"No way!"

"Right, and Janni knows that, so he's not expecting anything. Did you see the salad stuff that the old guy with the donkey gave me?"

"Yeah?"

"Well if I tried to pay him some money or buy him something he could be a bit offended, couldn't he."

JJ was deep in thought as he tried to work it all out.

"But there is a thing called poetic justice. Don't ask me what it means, but life has a habit of equalizing things. You know on the first morning in the coffee place after our swim, Janni's dad gave me that Greek coffee."

"You asked for that, didn't you?"

"Yeah, but he could have warned me."

"It was dead funny that!"

"Exactly. So you see what I mean?"

JJ, deep in thought, said, "I think so."

"Good. Cos I don't. Anyway, by the look of all the traffic we're nearly there."

"Oh, this is nice," said Molly, as they stepped off the bus.

What's nice about this? thought Jimmy, *Hundreds of cars and people.*

Molly, noticing Jimmy's expression, "Oh, come on! We haven't seen the shops all week."

JJ pointed towards the harbour, "Can we go and have a look at the boats?"

"Well, we're going to have a look at the shops. What are you going to do?"

"Let's go and have a look at the boats, Dad."

"Yeah, well we'll go and have a look at the boats – and that rock thing, a fort is it? Shall we, Billy?"

"Yeah, sure," Billy was his usual easy-going self.

"What are you doing, Mam? Are you coming to the shops with me and Sinead?"

Gran whispered to Sinead, "Why don't you go to the shops with your mam – it'll give you a chance to have a talk."

"What about?"

"I'm sure you'll think of something."

"No, I'm going with this lot," said Gran. "Keep them out of trouble."

"Right, OK. We'll meet you back here – what shall we say, twelve-thirty? No, make it one o'clock. Is that OK, Mam? OK, Sinead, it's me and you – let's go and have a look at the shops."

Molly wasn't surprised; Daisy never was one for the shops, though she'd been talking more and more as the week went on. The holiday was having an effect on them all in one way or another.

"Which boat are you going to have, Billy?" asked JJ as they got near the harbour.

"That one. That one over there, see?"

"Which one do you want, Dad?"

"I think I'll have that one," pointing to the one that just happened to have a young woman washing down the woodwork. Then, realising what he'd just said, he looked up to the sky and whispered, "I'm only kidding really."

The rock had an old cannon emplacement pointing out to sea, a reflection of days gone by. When JJ was out of earshot, Jimmy said to Billy and Daisy, "I just want to have a few minutes with the lad, if you can make yourselves scarce for a bit."

One of them days, thought Daisy.

"See these cannons, lad? Imagine the weight of this one here."

"Yeah, I bet you couldn't pick that up, could you Dad?"

"Couldn't budge it. These things are made out of what they call cast iron, and the way they did it – they got a giant mould, just like a jelly mould. You know when your mum's making a jelly she pours the hot jelly into a jelly mould and puts it in the fridge, and when it's set it comes out just like the shape of the mould."

"Yeah, I know, Dad – we've got a rabbit one."

"That's right. Well, these guns, these cannons are made in exactly the same way. You get the iron so hot that it melts and becomes a liquid, and then you pour it into a mould and when it's cooled down that's the shape it comes out. So just feel how hard and heavy this is." He picked him up so he could stand on the carriage. "Now imagine how hot it had to get to make that melt. So, what I was wanting to say… you know, about our little secret from the other day, if fire can melt that, imagine what it could do to plastic… So Danny Pritchard was wrong – plastic will burn, but when it does it melts and it can be very dangerous. So if fire can melt this, it can burn pretty well anything, can't it."

"Yeah, it can, can't it Dad."

"So that's how dangerous fire can be, so you must be very careful mustn't you."

"Yes, I will, Dad. I've never done it again."

"Good lad. And knives can also be very dangerous but, because I trust you, I'm going to give you your knife back – but keep it in your pocket and don't show it to anyone until I've told your mam. But give me it back tonight and I'll keep it safe until we get back home. Is that OK, lad?"

* * *

Sinead and Molly were sitting on a bench in a garden area. Sinead had been crying and Molly had her arms around her.

"I must admit, I did wonder, love."

"How did you know?"

"Mothers are supposed to know things like that, aren't they? And in any case it's not the first time this has ever happened, you know. Have you decided what you want to do?"

"Terry wants to have the baby, but I wasn't sure. But I do want to have the baby, Mam, I want to have my little baby. We want to get married." Sinead started to weep again. "But… me dad. Don't tell me dad, will you? I'm dreading him finding out."

"But he's got to know, love, hasn't he? He's got to know sooner or later."

"Yeah, I know, Mam, but not yet."

"No, not here. We'll wait until we get home. Leave your father to me."

* * *

Sinead hugged Gran when they met up. They wandered through the town and managed to find a cafe in a quiet square away from the madding crowds somewhat, where they could sit outside for lunch.

Jimmy remembered about a small church Nikolas had told him about, St Spyridon. He asked the waitress did she know it; she did, and it happened to be nearby, so they went to see it. It was only small, tucked away, but he could see why Nikolas mentioned it. It was like stepping into Aladdin's cave: full of extravagance and splendour. He couldn't help wondering why a church had to be so… so… in order for people to get in touch with their god.

Everybody was deep in thought as they started the bus journey back. Molly tried to start light-hearted chat. "Look at this, Mam," she leaned over the seat behind her. "It's a scarf, beautiful isn't it? Pure silk. And I've bought a couple of bits for Betty's two – I'll show you later."

JJ took his knife out of his pocket when he thought his Dad wasn't looking and held it between his cupped hands. Jimmy nudged him, and he quickly put it away.

"Don't blame Danny Pritchard," his dad said quietly, "you know, about plastic not burning. He might have just been having a joke… or his dad might have told him something like that, not thinking he'd take it too serious. It might have just been a bit of a joke, you know? You know, because I was just having a bit of a joke, you know, about eating aubergines makes you a genius and that's where you get your genes from."

"Yes, I know you were, Dad. But it could be, couldn't it?"

A little while later, JJ was asleep, Billy and Gran were quiet and content with their own thoughts. Sinead was asleep with her head resting on her mum's shoulders. Molly opened her bag and looked at the third bottle, oil of roses, and took it out to smell it.

As they passed through a tunnel, Jimmy tried to look through the blackened window. There appeared to be an orange glow around his own reflection. He moved forward and back and the glow moved with him. He closed his eyes and tried to rest, but it wasn't happening. He opened his eyes again, still in darkness, and looked through the window. There appeared to be a circle of light above his head. He found himself trying to hold back tears as he tried to come to terms with what was happening to him – but what was it?

Chapter 12

Janni was waiting as the bus arrived back at Niko's.

"Can I go fishing now, Mam? Can I? Look, there's Janni! Can I? Can I?"

"No, it's a bit late now, isn't it."

"Ah hey, Mam! You said I could, and I haven't caught a fish all week. This is my last chance."

"Let him go, love," said Jimmy.

"Oh, OK then, but make sure you're back by seven. Seven o'clock, you hear?"

"I've got a feeling you're going to catch one," whispered Jimmy.

"So have I, Dad."

"Make sure you're back at seven!" shouted Molly as JJ ran off. "Seven o'clock, do you hear me?"

"Yeah!"

* * *

Daisy and Billy were sitting outside Niko's when JJ ran up carrying two fish swinging on a line.

"Look at this! Look at these! I caught them! I did!"

"That's fantastic – look at the size of them!" said Billy. "Bloody hell! But your mam's going a bit ape. It's twenty to eight. Get across and see her quick."

"Look at these, Gran!"

"I knew you'd do it, son. I tell you what – leave them with me – you go and tell your mam you're back."

JJ dashed off, "Mam! Dad! I've caught two fishes!"

Daisy handed the fish to Billy, "Now, go and give these to your mate Dimitri and tell him to serve them up tonight, all special."

"He's not 'my' ..."

"Just do it, quickly. Come on, before anyone else comes down."

"But they're not that big... and I don't know..."

Daisy gave him one of her looks.

"I'd better tell Jimmy where I'm going."

"Alright, then – be quick."

* * *

"Where's these fish, then?"

"Here, look," said Billy, "but we've got to get them off to the Acropolis. I've just been told they're on tonight's menu."

Jimmy realised right away it was on Daisy's instructions. "They're great, aren't they? Good on the lad, but Molly hasn't seen them."

"No time for that! Have you tried saying no to Daisy?"

"OK, let's go then. Do you think they'll do it?"

"We can give it a go."

"Yes, of course," said Dimitri, "but they're not very big. We can dress them up – some tomatoes, maybe, some lemon."

"How about some of those courgettes and baby marrows?" said Jimmy.

"They're the same thing," said Dimitri.

"Yeah, I knew that."

"Well, if you serve plenty of bread," said Billy.

"Yeah, five."

They both looked at Jimmy. "Why five?"

* * *

The family were all seated at the table. JJ was sitting, uncharacteristically quiet and still, staring towards the door that led from the kitchen. Dimitri entered carrying a big silver platter and announced, "These are very special fish caught by a very special fisherman."

Everybody clapped. JJ's proudest moment ever.

Dimitri served fish to everyone and there was still some fish left. Everybody tucked into the meal with gusto, washing it down with wine. A while later, Dimitri returned and served more fish to everybody… and there was still some left. Dimitri returned again, but now everybody was full, and there was still fish left on the platter. All the wine had gone. Jimmy nervously poured some water into his glass, and sighed with relief as he realised it was still water.

Chapter 13

The next morning, Molly was first up.

"Come on you lot! We've just about got time for a last swim if you hurry up."

There wasn't really any need to rush; the coach taking them back to the airport wasn't arriving until ten forty-five, but it doesn't do any harm to throw some urgency into it, or nothing gets done.

* * *

They were all outside Niko's, looking mournfully down the track, knowing when they saw the coach their holiday was over. Gabbie was saying goodbye to Billy – the girls still had another few days. Jenny walked over to talk to Jimmy.

"You gave up too easy, you know. I quite fancied you."

"What! ...Well, as a matter of fact, I'm coming back tomorrow."

She laughed. "Next time, maybe, Jimmy Downie! Maybe next time... Right now you have a lot of work to do."

How does she know my name? And what's this – I've got a lot of work to do? That's what Father Jakovis said.

The coach drew up.

"Come on! Let's get on you lot... and I'm talking to you, too, JJ."

"But Janni said he was going to come."

"Well we can't hold up the coach. Come on now, get on!"

"Here he is, Mam!" Janni came running up the track.

As Billy put the cases in the luggage compartment, Nikolas called Jimmy, "Come and have a look at this." He showed Jimmy a painting. It was a picture of an old man, a fisherman, with weathered face, white beard.

"Do you know who this is? I believe it's an old Welsh fisherman."

Jimmy looked at the picture. "No, no idea," although it looked vaguely familiar.

"I want you to have it."

"Me?" Jimmy was stunned.

"It'll fit in your suitcase, won't it?"

"Yeah, yeah… I don't know what to say. That's very kind…"

"You don't have to say anything. You're a good man, Jimmy."

I wish people would stop saying that and just give me the money. I hope he doesn't say I've got a lot of work to do.

"But I've got nothing to give you."

"Oh, well, perhaps you will one day. Maybe you'll write the book."

Jimmy wandered back to the coach, trying to stop himself becoming… but money was preying heavily on his mind.

"Come on, Jimmy, and get JJ!" shouted Molly.

JJ and Janni were standing face to face, like two world ambassadors finalising a treaty between their respective nations. They shook hands, and JJ climbed on to the bus.

"He wanted to give me his old fishing rod," he said as he passed his mum and dad, "but I told him I wouldn't be able to get it through the airport and on to the plane," and went and sat next to Billy. Jimmy and Molly looked gobsmacked.

"Was that our lad saying that?"

There was a line of people to see them off including Gabbie

and Jenny, Nikolas and Despina. Stavros arrived, smiling, and winked at Molly.

"Did he just wink at you?" said Jimmy.

"Don't be soft!"

Janni was holding the rod out to JJ. JJ squeezed past Billy to get by the window, and mouthed through the glass, "We'll be coming back… Defo."

Dimitri was there, and smiled at everyone. He looked at Billy with a slightly different smile.

As the coach pulled away, Father Jakovis walked by and waved at Jimmy. Jimmy waved back, thoughtfully.

JJ looked at Father Jakovis. "He looks a bit like Osama Bin Laden!"

Sinead, Molly and Gran in unison, "Shurrup, JJ!"

The coach pulled away, then it had to pull into the side as an old man with a donkey and a little dog walked by.

* * *

They managed to get two rows of three on the plane, one behind the other. As the plane roared towards its cruising height, one by one they drifted into their own worlds, each radically different from the world they had brought with them just a few days before. Is that all it was? Just a few days? Time is a highly questionable form of measurement, but in this attempt at realisation it's the only one we have. Three and a half hours, according to the captain, was the expected flying time. JJ should have got in two or three *are we nearly there yet*s by now, but instead he was just looking out of the small window – not at the clouds that rushed by, but the numerous little cameos that were stored in chaos order inside, there to be flicked through whenever the occasion for reflection would allow. But then they would reappear without any command from him at all.

Sinead had arrived in Corfu with the unbearable burden that no-one should be asked to carry and, although the burden was still there, she knew now she had the strength to carry it, with the knowledge that what she had decided to do was right. A tear crept into her eye as she pictured Terry's face when she told him.

Perhaps Billy's story is just beginning, so we'll leave it for now.

Molly had rediscovered the good-looking woman she always was, but who had been buried for years under the organisation of schools, making sandwiches, cleaning, chaotic mealtimes and the mountain of washing. She reached out and took hold of Jimmy's hand. He squeezed hers.

What about Jimmy? Where do we start? If we were to imagine his mind was bouncing around like a ping-pong ball we wouldn't be far wrong, and perhaps the person it bounced on mostly was Father Jakovis – but what, for Christ's sake, did it all mean? He recalled something that old Harry had said before he passed away, 'What's the point, Jimmy? I don't know what the bloody point of it all is.' Why did he say that? Why did he leave Jimmy with the impossible question?

And Daisy. She certainly became a little more vocal towards the end of the week, as she discovered new purpose, a new role in the scheme of things. Don't get me wrong, she's never going to join the ramblers' association or the local Am. Dram., though she would have been quite good. Neither would she bake two dozen mince pies for the WI. Not in this lifetime. But somebody had to keep this lot in order; was it to be Daisy? Perhaps it was – in the best tradition of the matriarch: strong, silent and not to be messed with.

A stewardess, having chosen a prominent place in the aisle, announced that Thomas Cook was very pleased that everybody had chosen to fly with them, then showed a short film about how Thomas Cook had risen from modest beginnings, etc. Then the stewardess went on to say how much Thomas Cook valued their opinions and feedback on the standard of their holiday. She then proceeded to walk up and down the aisle handing out questionnaires. Jimmy dismissed it, but Molly reached out and took one.

"What did you get that for? We didn't even stay at a Thomas Cook hotel."

"Oh, you didn't have to. Anyway, me and Sinead will fill it in." She passed it over the seat behind her for Sinead to look at.

The various questions were discussed over the back of the seat, with Jimmy wondering what was the point, until Sinead mentioned a little bit in the small print: *This information may be used to advise you of future promotions or passed to a third party. Tick here if you do not wish this.* Jimmy's ears pricked up. Why would they wish to keep this form once they had assessed the relevance? Why would they pass it on to a third party? His mind flashed back to the stewardess who had introduced it. There was something about her manner, the tone in which she delivered it; a bit patronising, he thought. It was a while later when Jimmy realised: that was probably why they wanted the questionnaire. It wasn't for the information on it; it was the name of a sucker who might fall for future promotions. He whispered this to Molly, who hadn't passed the form in yet. She took the form out of the pocket in the seat front of her and showed Jimmy where they'd ticked the box that declined. As the plane started its descent, the stewardess came round to collect the questionnaires. Molly got her form out of the pocket to hand it in, but changed her mind, folded it up and put it back in her handbag.

Chapter 14

Back home in Liverpool, Molly, Daisy and Sinead were in the living room.

"Whatever you decide… Look, love, whatever you decide to do, it'll be OK with us, won't it, Mam."

"Of course it will." Daisy got up and gave Sinead a hug, "Though I'm not sure I like the idea of being a great grandmother, though." She stood up and looked in the mirror. "Look at me – I'm still a chicken!"

Sinead laughed through her tears.

"What we can do, though," said Molly, "is talk it through. You were hoping to go to uni, weren't you."

"Yes, Mum, I was. But you didn't go, did you?"

"No, but perhaps I should have. I probably could have."

"Do you wish you had have done?"

"Well, if I had, I probably wouldn't have married your dad. I'd have had a better choice."

"You're not sorry you married Dad, are you, Mum?"

Molly saw the look of shock, "No, not for a minute."

Now Daisy gave Molly a look.

"No, not for a minute, but there have been the odd few hours."

Daisy was still looking.

"OK, more than a few hours… and there have been times

when I could bloody kill him. But no, not for a minute."

"That's the way I feel about Terry."

"Yeah, I know. I'm sure it is. Yeah, but you're only going to be seventeen when you have the baby. I was only nineteen when I had you. And there's a lot more to marriage than the lovey-dovey stuff, you know. There'll be times when all you'll see is a crying baby and dirty nappies, and you'll wonder."

"Did you regret it?"

"Mm… No, I didn't allow myself to." She looked at her mother, "Got that off you, didn't I."

Daisy nodded, "Sure did."

"Though I always thought I'd go back to it. Not college – that was boring – but dress designing. I was good at that."

"Why didn't you, Mam?"

"Got bogged down with the routine, I suppose."

"Still could," said Daisy, still looking in the mirror, wondering if she should cut her hair a bit.

"What, go back to college at my age? You're joking… What are you trying to do – Educate Rita? No thanks."

"Well, there's one thing that's clear."

"What d'you mean?"

"You've talked Sinead into having the baby, if she had any doubts – which she didn't."

"How have I done that?"

"D'you want to tell her, Sinead, or shall I?"

"You tell her, Gran," she said, half laughing, half crying.

"When you were telling her about the possible regrets, about missing uni and stuff, all she could think about was how much she'd regret it if she didn't have the baby." Daisy turned to Sinead, "Am I right?"

"Yes," she nodded through her tears.

Molly gave her a hug.

"Well, that's that settled, then."

"So it looks like we're planning a wedding, then, doesn't it?" Sinead beamed.

"Well, there we are, OK then… you just leave your dad to me. I'll tell him when the time's right."

* * *

They'd been back home a few days when Molly went to answer a knock at the door.

"There's a man here from the council asking for you, Jimmy. Says he wants to see our bathroom."

"Oh, shit. Tell him there's no-one in."

"I've just spoken to him, soft arse. What does he want?"

"Tell him you're the cleaner or something. Tell him…"

The man from the council had heard the talking, and walked in.

"Are you Mr Downie?" he said. "I hope you don't mind me walking in. My name is Gregory, from the council." He showed Jimmy his official pass. "I've come to inspect the bathroom."

"Bathroom? What d'you want to see our bathroom for?" said Molly.

"Leave it to me, love… Well it's not convenient right now. Can you call back?"

"Well… well no. I'd really like to see it now if I may. It won't take long. I've been twice already but there's been nobody in."

"Er, erm, well you can't just now, I'm afraid. Billy's in there."

"No he isn't, Dad," said JJ.

"Yes he is."

"No, I saw him going down the street."

"Well he came back. He needed to go to the toilet."

"What's all this about?" Molly asked the council man.

"Well, I do need to see it, Mr Downie – if you could check please."

"Well, I wouldn't just now if I was you. You see, since we got back from our holiday … Billy boy picked up a bit of a stomach bug, and… and… Well, I'd leave it for now, if you see what I mean."

"I'm sorry, Mr Downie, but I really must insist. You see it's my duty. I have the authority." He reached into his briefcase for the authorisation.

Jimmy focused all his will on Daisy. *Come on, Gran. I need you now.* "I've actually got the same bug myself and I need to get

97

into the bathroom as soon as Billy's finished." *Come on, Gran. Don't let me down.*

"I give up," said Molly, "I don't think I'm on the same planet any more," and went into the kitchen.

Daisy sighed, and smiled sweetly.

JJ pulled a handkerchief out of his pocket and tied it round his face, bandit-style.

The council man winced and muttered to himself, "Bloody hell!"

"Oh, excuse me. I beg your pardon," said Jimmy.

The council man checked his watch, "Well, I can't wait any longer. I've got another appointment. I'll have to go. I'll be back, Mr Downie."

Molly returned from the kitchen. "What the bloody hell was all that about?"

"It was just about the grant, I think."

"What grant?"

"The grant we got for the new bathroom."

"What are you talking about? We haven't got a new bathroom."

"You remember! We filled in all the forms, didn't we – to get a new bathroom."

"Yeah, but we never sent them off."

"Well, we did, actually. I didn't think we'd actually get it, but we did. And they paid us for it."

"How much?"

"Three grand."

"Bloody hell! Well, where's the money?"

"Erm… In Corfu."

JJ punched the air, "Nice one, Dad!"

"You go up to your room, JJ!"

"Are, eh, Mam!"

"Now!"

JJ knew when she must be obeyed.

Molly turned to her mother, "Did you know, Mam?"

Daisy remained silent.

"Did Billy know?"

"No, nobody knew."

"How the hell did you think you were going to get away with that?"

"I didn't think they'd check up – well, not so quick."

"Of course they check up! They're not stupid."

"Yeah, I know. I was going to tell you when we got back. Spend a few bob on it, get it done up."

"A few bob! What d'you call a few bob? How much have you got left?"

Jimmy opened his wallet and put one hundred and ten euros on the table and some change.

Molly stared from Jimmy to her mum in disbelief.

"You spent three grand on the holiday!"

"Apart from that," he said, nodding to the money on the table.

Daisy started to laugh.

"It's not funny, Mam! You told me you'd been saving up for the holiday for ages."

"When have you ever known me not be skint by Wednesday? Look, it's not that bad – I've got a hundred and thirty pounds in the bank."

"You think a hundred and thirty quid is going to look like three grand's worth of work?"

"That's about two hundred and thirty pounds," said Daisy, "with the euros."

"Don't you start taking his side, Mother! We've apparently got to get a new bathroom by tomorrow. New bath, new toilet, new shower…"

"And knock down the wall between the bathroom and the toilet."

"Oh God! This is your best one yet!"

Jimmy thought for a tiny moment about telling her how good the holiday was, but stopped himself.

* * *

Back at work, and Charlie Madden was not very happy.

"He's a bit of a sore arse, isn't he?" said Jimmy over the morning break.

"Ah, don't worry about it. He'll come round. It's not your fault the stitcher broke down while we were away."

"Well, to be honest, I'm not surprised. I knew it was going to overrun before we went, but I just didn't have time to change the tracker slide."

"Yeah, I know, but he knew that, didn't he?"

"Yes, he bloody knew – I told him weeks ago, but try telling him that now."

"Ah, don't worry about it, mate. He'll come round."

"Yeah, but I need him to be the Jolly Roger. The shit hit the fan a bit after we got back."

"Like what?"

"I'll tell you later, can't tell you now. Let's go for a pint in the Duck House after work, and I'll tell you then."

* * *

That evening in the Duck House (the pub was actually called The Flying Geese, but nobody called it that – it was probably because of its close proximity to the lake), Jimmy told Billy the whole bathroom-council thing. Billy knew when there were times when the bloody obvious didn't need saying. He could see Jimmy was suffering quite enough without him rubbing salt into the wound.

"…So I was thinking of tapping Charlie, but that's a non-starter."

"Oh, he'll come round. Did you get the stitcher going?"

"Yeah, but he's never been big on lending money, has he? He knocked Danzie back last month, didn't he."

"It's the council, Jimmy, not the mafia. They're not going to stick a horse's head in your bed. We've just got to get the bathroom done."

"What about the council fellah? He's supposed to be coming back tomorrow."

"Well tell him to piss off. Tell him you need a couple of weeks. It's the council, Jimmy. It takes them two weeks just to put a piece of paper in an envelope. Look, they're doing up them houses in Handcroft Street, aren't they? They don't care when they go in, they just rip everything out and replace it. They're bound to be throwing some good stuff out."

It was unusual for Billy to play the big brother, but that's what mates do when it's necessary.

* * *

The next morning, Molly answered the phone.

"Good morning. Mrs Downie? This is Liverpool City Council here."

Her heart sank.

"I'm phoning to apologise. Mr Gregory is supposed to be visiting you today, but I'm afraid he's been taken ill. He'll have to make another appointment. I hope we haven't inconvenienced you."

"Oh, I'm sorry to hear that, but I did have to rearrange my schedule. How long is he likely to be off?"

"Yes, I apologise again. It's likely to be a couple of weeks – some sort of stomach problem."

Molly put the phone down. "Did you hear that, Mam? The council fellah's got a stomach problem and can't make it."

"Hmm," said Daisy. "Since when did you have a schedule?"

***

After work the next evening Jimmy and Billy walked towards the skip in Handcroft Street.

"At least we've got a couple of weeks." Jimmy had told Billy about the council guy catching a mysterious stomach bug.

They stopped at the skip and examined a bath sticking out of the top.

"Hey, Billy, this isn't bad."

"Nah, it's no good. It's got a lump knocked out of the corner here, look."

"Oh, crap! I bet they did that dumping it into the skip. You'd think they'd take more care."

"They've got another skip down at the end of the street. Let's go and have a look at that one." They started walking.

"Well, whatever, I've got to come up with something. We could start knocking down the wall or something. Could you give us a lift this weekend?"

"No, can't this weekend, mate. I'm actually going back to Corfu for a couple of days."

"What!"

"I've been meaning to tell you, but with all the council crap I haven't had a chance."

"Tell me what? Why are you going back to Corfu? I might come with you – Molly's going mad."

"Well…" Billy hesitated, "I think I've found somebody I'd like to spend a bit of time with."

"What?" The penny dropped. "You sly dog! That Gabrielle! I knew it – I knew you were at it!"

"No, no, not Gabbie."

"Jenny? You don't mean Jenny!"

"No, I don't mean Jenny."

"Who, then?"

"Well, you know that taverna we used to go to, the Acropolis?"

"Yeah, of course I do. It wasn't that long ago."

"And the waiter, Dimitri – you know the guy who looked after us?"

"Yeah?"

"Well," Billy paused.

It dawned on Jimmy what Billy was trying to say. "Oh, Jesus Christ, Billy! You're fucking joking! Hang on a minute, Billy, are you taking the piss? I mean he's a raving …"

They walked past the skip towards the park. Jimmy's mind was crammed with confusion. He kept trying to form the words to tell Billy what he thought, but all the came out was, "You can't, you see… because… Let's just weigh this up for a minute."

They weighed it up for about half an hour. Having given it much thought, Jimmy blurted, "Is there anyone on Corfu you didn't give one to?"

Billy shouted, just as an elderly couple walked by, "I didn't give her one!"

Jimmy and Billy walked around the lake in silence. They found some bread on the ground to feed the ducks.

"No wonder the goats were nervous when you were around!"

"Too fucking right!"

They both burst out laughing. They'd walked completely round the lake twice. They passed the same old couple now sitting on a bench.

"You did give Gabbie one, didn't you? Then she knocked you back. That's what happened, wasn't it?"

"I didn't give her one, Jimmy!"

The old man, looking thoughtful, turned to his wife and whispered, "I wouldn't mind giving it one."

"Hmmm."

They got up and started to walk towards the exit of the park, getting quicker and quicker as they went.

Jimmy and Billy walked home in silence. They got to the corner and stopped.

"When are you going?"

"Friday. Midnight. Back Sunday, late."

"You'll be going to work on Monday, then, won't yer?"

"Yeah, course I will – it's only for a weekend. Nothing's changed."

But it had. Could it ever be the same again? Jimmy felt drained.

* * *

Molly was in the living room when Jimmy walked in.

"Bloody hell, Moll! I've just had the shock of my life. Billy's just told me he's going back to Corfu."

"I'm not entirely surprised."

"What I'm trying to tell you... He's going back to Corfu... He wants to see that Dimitri – you know, the poofter."

"OK, well tea's nearly ready."

"Are you listening? What I'm trying to tell you is Billy boy's gay."

"Yes, I know. Bless him."

"Hang on a minute. You knew he was gay?"

"Of course I did. I've known for years."

Jimmy looked around to see if the wallpaper and the ornaments on the mantelpiece were as stunned as he was. "I mean..." trying to emphasise the point, "He's going back to Corfu this weekend to see Dimitri, that gay guy in the Acropolis – the guy..." Jimmy waltzed around the living room with his hand on his hip.

Molly chuckled, "Oh, you do it much better than him. And while you're waltzing around go and tell me mam dinner's nearly ready, and call the kids."

"Dinner's ready? Since when did we start calling it dinner?"

"Since our holidays. Everybody called it dinner there, and it sounded so much... Well, anyway, that's what it is from now on. Now go and call the kids."

Jimmy turned towards the door.

"Now don't mention it to the kids. We'll talk about it later. I'll be able to talk him out of it, I'm sure, it's just a bit of a whim. I mean, there's so much of it on telly isn't there."

Later that evening, "I don't blame him. He's a good looking man that Dimitri... and Stav..." Molly stopped herself just in time. "Dimitri has got such a wicked sense of humour."

"When did you find out about his wicked sense of humour?"

"That night when you went beddie-byes on the sunbed

outside the Apollo. Me and Billy had a drink with him at the Acropolis."

"I'll have you know I had a very stressful day that day. I'm surprised Billy didn't tell you all about it."

"No, not a word," said Molly, with a mischievous grin. "He was just staring into Dimitri's eyes."

"Oh, shurrup, will you." Jimmy thought for a few moments. "Is there anything else you know that I don't?"

"Bumble bee."

"Bumble bee? What the fuck's bumble bee got to do with anything?"

Molly changed the subject quickly. "Sinead's pregnant."

"Pregnant? Pregnant? I bet it was that Greek bastard. That bloody Greek bastard. I'll fucking kill him!"

"Don't be stupid! Maths was never your strong point, was it, Jimmy? How long have we been back?"

Jimmy's mind raced back to Corfu. His head felt like it was exploding. So many things, so much had happened, in those few days.

There was a Crack!, as if something had snapped, and then the house went black, jet black – but it wasn't just the house; it was as though the whole world had gone black and silent. It was just for a moment but seemed like an age… then the light returned.

"What the hell was that?"

Molly didn't answer. She just stood there, silent, still, staring.

"Molly!! Molly?"

No reply.

Then a voice boomed out.

"Jimmy Downie!"

He jumped.

"Jimmy Downie, you are banished to the Wilderness."

PART 2

THE WILDERNESS

Chapter 15

When the light returned, Jimmy was sitting on a boulder in the middle of a barren landscape. No life. No living room. No Molly. No nothing.

"Do you know where you are, Jimmy Downie?"

Jimmy looked round. *I'm dreaming*, he thought, *I'm just dreaming… but I'm not asleep… but that's it.*

"Do you know where you are, Jimmy Downie?" the voice repeated.

"Hello?" said Jimmy.

"Hello," replied the voice, "Do you know where you are?"

He began to move around to see where the voice was coming from. "Where am I?"

"I asked first," said the voice.

Now he knew it was all a dream he wasn't so nervous. "I've seen this place before – it's Old Trafford, isn't it."

The voice tried to suppress a laugh. "Think again, Jimmy Downie. I've given you a clue. Well, in actual fact I've said it."

"What, the Wilderness, you mean?"

"Got it in one... well, it was actually two. Now why do you think you're in the Wilderness?"

"I'm dreaming. Dreams are weird. It's a dream, isn't it?" his voice echoed back.

Voice, anxious to move things along a bit, said, "You must mend your evil ways, Jimmy Downie... and no, you're not dreaming."

Jimmy was beginning to realise that... He wasn't dreaming.

Voice, a bit impatient at the lack of progress, said, "Have you come to repent your evil ways?" Then he corrected himself, "You have come to repent your evil ways, haven't you."

"Yes. I'm terribly sorry. I didn't mean it."

"Good. What are you sorry about?"

"I'm not sure really."

"Have a good think, Jimmy Downie. Is there nothing you want to be forgiven for?"

Jimmy had a long hard think. "Oh, I know what it is... it's about Billy Boy, isn't it."

"What about Billy Boy?"

"Well it's my fault isn't it. It's my fault he's gay isn't it? It's all my fault."

"How d'you work that out?"

"Well I was always pushing him, wasn't I, you know, to get girlfriends. I should have let him alone, he'd have found a girlfriend when he was ready."

"That's rubbish. I made him gay, or rather we did."

"You made him gay?"

"Don't sound so surprised. We've got to keep our quotas up, you know. What is it? One in ten or one in fifteen? I'm not sure. It keeps changing."

"You've got to keep your quotas up?"

"Stop repeating everything I say. We won't get anywhere."

"But quotas? What are you talking about, quotas?"

"Gays. What is it? One in ten, one in fifteen? It varies. He calls it sending in a curved ball."

"He? Who the hell is he?"

"That's an unfortunate phrase, but you're right. I shouldn't call him He. I must apologise for that. He hates it when I call him He, and I don't blame Him. Bad manners. The Big Guy… God."

* * *

Back in the living room, Molly was talking with her mother.

"How the hell are we going to get that bathroom sorted?"

"Well, there's that builder, George Cooper. Remember..? He did some work for me and your dad, a few years ago."

"Oh, that's right. He sorted out your front bay, didn't he? That was OK, wasn't it?"

"Eventually, but he jumped the price up. Watch him."

"Yes, right. He knows Jimmy. Anyway, I'll give him a call. I've got his number somewhere…" She went through the drawer, pulled out an old scrap of paper, and dialled.

"Good morning, Mr Cooper. It's Molly here, Molly Downie,

Jimmy's wife. I need a bit of building work doing. New bathroom suite and a wall taking down...

..."No, next month's no good. I need it doing right away...

..."Oh, come on, George. Jimmy's always helped you...

..."He helped you get the cat out of the tree, didn't he...

..."Oh, come on, he never hurt it...

..."They weren't bricks, they were only small stones. You can't blame him for that...

..."That cat always had a limp – and what about that time he towed your car?

..."Well, the bumper couldn't have been fixed on proper, could it?

..."Well, if it was a BMW it should have been fixed proper in the first place, shouldn't it?

..."Ah, come on, George. By the way, did the Legion ever find out what happened to that hundred and fifty quid out of the Christmas fund?

..."Ah, thanks, George. I'll see you first thing Monday. Oh, and I want your best trade prices – I'm not bloody made of money."

Molly put the phone down. "I've got to stop swearing... but it's that George Cooper, he gets to me, he's a slime ball. So anyway he's coming first thing Monday, but apparently he can't do the plastering or the electrics."

* * *

Jimmy continued his conversation with Voice.

"It's our Sinead, isn't it? I'll kill that bastard."

"Mind your language, Jimmy Downie."

"Oh, sorry. I'm very sorry."

"Only joking. Anyway, what about your Sinead?"

"She's pregnant, isn't she? That Greek bas.... I mean that

Greek chappie. I should have kept a closer eye on her. I should have been looking after her. I'll bloody kill the bastard."

"Maths was never your strong point, was it Jimmy? How long have you been back from Corfu? A week, is it? Nearly two weeks now."

"That's right. Yeah, about that."

Jimmy started to work out the maths…

"You mean it wasn't Corfu? So it wasn't the Greek get? Who was it then..? Terry. Was it her boyfriend Terry? I thought he was a decent lad."

"He is a good lad. So, it's not your Sinead you need to repent about."

Darkness started to fall on the first day in the Wilderness.

"I'm not doing very well, am I? How long have I got to be here for?"

"It's usually the best part of two days."

"Oh, is that all? Thank Christ for that."

"That's right."

"Oh, excuse me. I didn't mean… I just thought it might have been forty days and forty nights."

"Oh the bible stuff you mean? I didn't believe that, did you? I think they upped the figures to forty days and forty nights to make it a bit more dramatic. I think a bit of theatre crept in, don't you? Anyway, back to business."

"It's not me swearing is it? I don't mean anything."

"No, of course not. You want to hear this lot up here."

* * *

Molly was on the phone again.

"Hiya, AC. How're you doing?

"…I need a bit of sparking doing, mate…

…"No, that's no good – it's got to be Tuesday, Tuesday morning…

..."No, that's no good either. The plastering's getting done Tuesday afternoon. It'll only take you an hour if you pull your finger out... Speaking of that, you're not in the Church choir any more, are you? Didn't you leave quite quickly?

..."Cheers AC/DC! I'll see you Tuesday."

Molly put the receiver down, then picked it up again and dialled another number.

"Hiya Bongo? Molly Downie here. How are you doing?

..."Look, I need a bit of plastering doing and a bit of tiling. How're you fixed?

..."No. Tuesday. It's got to be Tuesday... or Wednesday latest...

..."Well, I think you'd better cancel that, Bongo. I need the plastering done Tuesday...

..."That's no good Bongo. That's too late. Jimmy's in a spot of bother... By the way, does your Mary know about that slag in Acacia Street?

..."Two o'clock Tuesday? That'll do nicely. See you then."

Molly put the phone down. "God, I feel like bleedin' Anneka Rice!"

* * *

Back in the Wilderness.

"It's not Man U is it – it's not badmouthing Man U, is it?"

"No, we all do that."

Jimmy was sitting on his boulder, resting his head in his hands, struggling to think.

"The bathroom, is it?" He looked up.

"Now you're getting warm at last."

"Not the grant for the new bathroom?"

"That's it Jimmy, now you've got it, at last."

"I've been sent to the Wilderness because I've fiddled a bit of poxy grant off the poxy council for a new poxy bathroom? That's a bit harsh, isn't it?"

"Yes, well, I think you're right. I must admit I agree with you, but I've been falling down on my targets lately and so I'm under a bit of pressure."

"Targets… You've got targets?"

"Oh, yes."

"You've got targets for sending people to the Wilderness?"

"Yes, of course we do. How else d'you think we get people motivated? But the targets they set these days are ridiculous. Six Wildernesses a month. I blame New Labour. Anyway, we're sorted now. All you've got to do is promise not to do it again, and we can let you off with a warning this time. How's that? But I must rush you… I've just noticed the time. I'm off to a bit of a do tonight. One of the archangels is having a bit of a party and there's loads of fairies going – and between you and me they're gagging for it."

"Fairies? Gagging for what?"

"Oh, they're not the ones you're thinking of. These are the ones with the gossamer wings and some of them are… anyway, I haven't got time now."

"I don't believe this. Anyway, alright, I promise. I promise whatever you like. I'm out of here. You said I was only going to be here for two days."

"Yeah, well it's two days from Monday."

"When's Monday?"

"It was two days ago in your time. A couple of bits before you go: how long have you known Billy boy?"

"Ten… no, more… fifteen years."

"Exactly. He's still the same lad you know, and he's going to come in for a bit of stick. Oh, and by the way your favourite colour is avocado. Oh, and one more thing, you are the Disciple."

"You what?" Jimmy shouted.

"My fault, should have told you earlier. That's the main reason you're here. You see, the main man, God, has been a bit pissed off lately. You know, the world is rife with greed and corruption, and the priests and vicars are doing precious little to stop it. It seems like half of them are as bad, or turning out to be perves or child molesters, so anyway, we're going for the radical alternative. Anyway, in a nutshell, the Big Guy called all us archangels together – big meeting, sort of thing. Anyway, in another nutshell, he told us to come up with the radical alternative… disciple sort of thing. And, er… anyway, I suggested you."

"Oh, thanks very much! Why me?"

"Sorry Jim, I'd been on the moon juice."

"Oh, that'd work."

"You haven't had moon juice have you?"

"Well, yeah, we call it Stella."

"I haven't tried Stella. D'you reckon it's as good as moon juice?"

"Better…" *I don't believe I just said that.*

"You won't have to – you'll forget most of this by the time you get home. Look, got to go now. Look forward to seeing you again soon."

"Wish I could say the same," muttered Jimmy.

Jimmy was wondering how he was going to tell people where he'd been for the last few days.

"Don't worry about that," said Voice, who apparently could read his thoughts. "They won't know you've been missing. Just remember – you're the chosen one."

"What?"

* * *

The phone rang and Daisy answered it.

"Can I speak to Mrs Downie, please? George Cooper here."

"She's out at the moment. Can I take a message?"

"Oh, well, er, it's about some work she's asked me to look at."

"Yes, I know about that. You're coming round on Monday to do it."

"Ah, well, you see, that's why I'm calling. It's going to be a couple of weeks before I can get to it."

"No! Monday was the arrangement and that's when it wants doing."

"Well, perhaps I should speak to Mrs Downie. When d'you think she'll be back?"

Daisy felt her hackles rise. She didn't like him. Her fuse was beginning to burn down. "NO! Perhaps you tell me. What's the problem?"

"No problem as such, not as such. But it's about the price. Am I right in thinking what I might have heard, erm… Is it true, er… Mr Downie might have received a council grant for this work?"

She exploded, "Now listen, Cooper. That job is going to be done on Monday. By you…

…"Shurrup, I haven't finished yet. And you will finish by midday Tuesday…

…"Well, you'd better put another man on it, then…

…"Don't interrupt, I haven't finished… I'm glad you mentioned the council. You got that job off the council for the new leisure centre, didn't you? That job didn't go to tender, did it? You gave them a backhander, didn't you?"

No response.

"And one more thing – when the job's finished, midday Tuesday, and all the rubbish is cleared up, you will forget to raise a bill…

..."Shurrup! Because if you don't, I'll stick your head on a pole so the whole of Liverpool can throw stones... and what your cat got will seem like nothing."

Daisy put the phone down and looked at it. She was shaking. She went to the kitchen and put the kettle on. By the time she'd poured her cup of tea her hands were steady. She sat in her favourite chair, closed her eyes and drifted off to the Mississippi. She smiled – not the smile that went with the stomach problem, but the smile of contentment that went with a job well done.

Harry would have enjoyed that, she thought. But then she knew he was watching anyway, he was never far away...

"*The girl's back in town!*"

Chapter 16

Jimmy arrived home and walked in sheepishly.

"Hiya, love. How are you doing? Look I'm sorry, love, I've been a bit of a bloody idiot, haven't I?"

"You can say that again, you soft get. Come on, have a cup of tea." She walked into the kitchen to put the kettle on.

"What made you do it?"

"I didn't think we'd get caught. It seemed a good idea at the time. I did do it for the family. I thought we deserved a proper holiday."

"We always do have proper holidays."

"Yes, I know – but North Wales. I wanted us to go abroad. You hear the lads talking down the pub. I was saving up, but then the boiler broke down, didn't it. And then your mam moving in."

"Well, that didn't cost anything."

"No, I know. Just a bit of decorating, wasn't it. But then the car – three hundred and fifty quid to get it through the M.O.T. There was always something. Anyway, things are going to change. I've been doing a lot of thinking."

"So have I. Go and have a look upstairs while I make the tea."

Jimmy came back down. "That's my favourite colour, avocado."

"Well, it's not mine. It's a bit old fashioned, but it's not bad, is it?"

The bathroom was perfect: wall down, tiling finished, painted. Jimmy didn't know what to say – nothing seemed to make sense any more. All he could say was, "Don't underrate avocado."

"Here, have your cup of tea."

"Speaking of North Wales, where did you put my picture – the one Nikolas gave us?"

"Upstairs. Needs framing."

"No it doesn't. I like it the way it is. A famous Welsh fisherman, he said. No idea who, though. Have you?"

"Thought I did. He does look vaguely familiar. Like the face off a sardine can or something."

"Yeah, I know what you mean, but it's not that. Might take it to the Walker Art Gallery. They'll know."

"Well, they probably will. It's a good picture."

"The disciples were fishermen, weren't they?"

"What made you say that?"

"Don't know. How's Sinead?"

"She's OK. We'll talk about it later."

* * *

Molly and Daisy were in the living room.

"When are you going to tell him about the wedding?"

"Well, tonight, I suppose. I'm sure he's half expecting it, but weddings are very expensive – he'd have worked that out too."

"Waste of money if you ask me."

"Oh, she's got it all worked out: three bridesmaids, a church… I bet she's thinking about a reception in some posh hotel and all, but she daren't mention that because she knows what I'd say."

"You were exactly the same, you know."

"I was not!"

"Oh yes you were. Me and your dad had no money either, you know."

"I made my bridesmaids' dresses, didn't I, with a little bit of help from Dorothy Perkins."

"Well, do it again."

"Christ! I haven't sewn anything for years... and she'd never wear anything out of Dorothy Perkins."

"Well, there's loads of other shops. Top Cat, Top Shop, whatever it's called."

"Oh, she won't have that. She'll want something out of the brides' shops. It'll cost hundreds, thousands probably... and the cake."

"The cake? The cake's a bloody cake! Look, leave Sinead to me. I'll tell her how we went through exactly the same thing when you got married, and how you made the dresses and stuff. By the time we've had a chat – probably two chats – she'll be chuffed to death that her mum's designing her wedding dress, and you two go off down town, have a good look at all the shops, get basic dresses, then you get yourself sewing again and make them look magic with some curtain material or something."

"You can't use curtain material!"

"No, I don't mean curtain material. I mean proper decent stuff. There's a few fabric shops down by the side of TJs, isn't there. You know where I mean, you've been there loads of times."

Molly's head was spinning. "It's still going to take money."

"Look, I've got a bit put aside... and I've got a bit of pension coming in, haven't I, that I'm not using since I moved in here – and a bit of insurance coming in off your dad."

"Oh, I wish my dad was here, Mam," said Molly, and started to fill up.

"Oh, don't you bloody start and all! Look, your dad's looking down on us, isn't he, and he's going to make sure we get it sorted, isn't he. Your dad thought the world of Jimmy, you know."

"Yes, I know he did."

"Now go and wipe your face. JJ's going to be home in a minute… look at the time."

"Oh God! JJ. That's another thing. It's his birthday soon. Every day he's on about getting a fishing rod. They've got them in the catalogue and he's seen them."

"That's going to be a five minute wonder. He's not going to want to get up at six o'clock in the morning in the middle of winter in Liverpool to catch worms… and sit on a wet bank in the pouring rain, when all he's going to catch is a shopping trolley or a pram."

* * *

It was early evening. Molly and Jimmy were in the lounge of a nearby pub, one that they didn't go to too often, so they could talk.

"How's Billy?"

"Oh, he's OK."

"I mean how did his weekend go?"

"I haven't really seen him to talk to too much today."

Molly knew they were inseparable at break times and lunch times at work.

"How long has Billy been your mate, Jimmy? Fifteen years? He's still the same lad, you know, and he's going to come in for a bit of stick."

Jimmy looked around. It had happened again. He got a flash of memory of his time in the Wilderness when the voice had said exactly the same thing. "Yeah, I know, it just came as a bit of a shock. Now I've had a chance to think, I see what you mean. Dimitri is a good-looking lad, isn't he."

"Hey, don't you start getting ideas! Look, we need to talk about Sinead. Me and me mam have had a good chat with Sinead, and she's a good kid, you know."

"No! Is she? I didn't know that. I think I know what you're going to tell me – she wants to get married, doesn't she."

"Well, yeah," Molly sighed with relief.

"I'm not entirely surprised. Well, what do you think?"

"She's got her heart set on it."

"Well, they have been going out for quite a while, now, haven't they. They should know each other a bit..." Jimmy paused to think and had a swig of his beer. "How can I say no? Can't really, can I? Terry does seem a decent lad..."

"Terry is a decent lad."

"Don't think much of his old feller, though, do you?"

"Yes, I know, but Terry's not like him... She's been terrified of telling you, you know."

"God! Am I that much of an ogre?"

"No you're not. Not quite. Anyway, I need another drink." Molly went to bar, glad that it was now all out in the open, and returned with a pint and a half of lager. "... And the other thing is, of course, the cost of the wedding. They're bloody expensive."

"Can't they run off to Gretna Green or something?"

"Oh, come on, I know you don't mean that. She's your only daughter."

"Don't I?"

"Look, they want to do it properly: church, bridesmaids, the lot."

"Christ!" Jimmy looked up at the ceiling by way of apology.

"They've been thinking about this for a long time. She knew before our holiday, you know," Molly saw Jimmy's reaction, "and don't say why didn't you know before. You know now... and, Jimmy Downie, as prospective father of the bride, Terry's coming round to ours tonight at eight o'clock," she looked at her watch, "in about three quarters of an hour, to ask you for your permission to marry her."

"Is he? Is he? That takes a bit of bottle."

* * *

Promptly at eight o'clock there was a knock on the door and Terry came in.

"Hello Mr Downie. I wonder if I could just, er… I wonder if we could, er… If you're not too busy…"

"Yeah, of course you can, lad. Come in." He turned to Molly and Sinead. "Look this is man's talk. You two in the kitchen. Alright? …Right Terry, lad. Come and sit down and, by the way, it's Jimmy… OK lad, fire away."

"Well, it's me and Sinead. You see Mr…er Jimmy, we're going to be parents."

"So I've heard, lad, but I like the way you put it. So I hear you both want to have the baby?"

"I love her, Mr Downie… er, Jimmy. And I think she loves me, and we really want to get married."

"Love is a very big word, lad. Said very quickly."

"I do. I do love her. I missed her when she was away. I wanted to be there to look after her."

"Aye, I know. You're not a bad lad, Terry. How d'you propose looking after her?"

"Well I'm nineteen now, and in another twelve months I'll be on full money, and there's plenty of work, and I'm going to do foreigners, and I'm doing foreigners now, and people say I do good work, and we want to have our own house, and…"

"Slow down lad! You'll be no good to her if you have a heart attack."

"I think I have already, Mr Downie… Will you let us get married?"

"Where d'you intend living, mate?"

"Well, we could live at ours till we find our own place, but me old fellah can be a bit…"

"Yeah, I know lad. I know your dad. He can be a bit of a handful sometimes. So are you asking me can you move in here?"

"No no, I wasn't asking that, Mr Downie. Well, unless you think…"

There was a knock on the front door. The girls came out of the kitchen and Molly went to answer it. Sinead whispered to Terry.

"What's he said? Has he agreed?"

"I don't know."

"It's Billy, Jimmy," said Molly.

"Come in Billy."

Billy entered carrying a suit he'd borrowed ages ago.

"You'd better hang on to that Billy boy, seeing there's going to be a wedding. But throw it over the chair for now 'cos you and me are going out for a pint – and you better come as well, Terry lad, seeing you're going to be part of the family."

"Can I come, Dad?" said JJ.

"No, not this time, lad," Jimmy looked at Molly.

"No! No, he can't," she said.

Terry, Jimmy and Billy went off to the pub.

Sinead threw her arms round Molly and cried, and so did Molly.

Sinead started dancing round the room, singing,

"I love my daddy,
you know I do,
I love my daddy,
and that's the truth.."

JJ put the television on and lay on the floor looking at fishing rods in the catalogue, but mainly to get in Sinead's way to stop her dancing around.

* * *

Jimmy, Billy and Terry were in the Duck House.

"Well, that's great, that is. What a bloody week! Me best mate gay, and me future son in law an Evertonian – I don't know what's worse."

"An Evertonian," said Billy without hesitation.

"Yeah, you're probably right. So, Terry, you're working on the building?"

"Yeah, joiner, on the hospital."

"Big job, that, isn't it?" said Billy.

"Yeah, another three or four years, they reckon."

"Didn't you used to do a bit of boxing and all, at one time?" asked Jimmy.

"Yeah, in me school days. I thought about taking it up for a while, but there's no future in it… didn't do me dad any good."

"Hey, well here's a thought," said Jimmy, "just a thought, mind. Would you know how to go about doing up the loft in our house? I wondered about doing that a while back, didn't I, Billy? A few of the houses in the street have done it."

"Yeah, I could do that. No problem. One of the lads in work has done his loft. I can get him to give us a lift."

"Well, hang on a minute, it's just a thought. Don't get carried away."

"I'm an Evertonian, Jimmy – I'm used to getting carried away."

"Ha, ha, ha, ha!"

"He's not a bad lad, this, is he, considering he's an Evertonian."

Terry stood up to go and get some more beer. "Is that lager, Billy?"

"No, we're alright for a moment," said Jimmy, "and you'd better get back and see our Sinead. She'll be having kittens. Just sit down for a minute – you've got a bit left. Have you ever been fishing?"

"Yeah, years ago when I was a kid."

"Because our Jimmy won't stop talking about it, and it's his birthday coming up, and he's after a fishing rod, and I haven't got a clue."

"The one I've got wasn't expensive, but that was a few years ago. He can have that one, if you want. I don't bother these days."

"Where did you used to go?" asked Billy.

"The best place is North Wales. I went with our Tony and his mate. He had a car. But I can't remember whereabouts."

"Alright, pal. Well, cheers for that. You'd better get back... and no word about the loft thing until we've had a chance to talk it through. OK, mate?"

"Yeah, of course."

Terry left.

"It's a good trade, a chippy, isn't it. I always thought that was the best one on the building. Never could understand how electricity got from one end to the other. Used to fancy doing a bit of joinery myself one time."

"Whatever happened to those coffee tables you made?"

"Gave them away. Good, though, weren't they. Spalted beech, some of them... and I did a few sculptures with the offcuts – remember that?"

"Whatever happened to them?"

"Oh, they're up in the loft somewhere. Look, mate. I'm sorry about being a bit off the other day. It was just, well, a bit of a shock, I suppose."

"Don't worry about it, Jim. I'll have to get used to that."

"So, how did the weekend go?"

"Yeah, it was good. Jenny was asking about you."

"Was she?"

"No, soft arse! She was probably back in Rochdale weeks ago!"

"Oh, yeah, of course." Jimmy struggled to find the words, "Er, how long have you been, erm…"

"Gay, you mean? You can say it, Jimmy."

"Well, yeah."

"Ever since they started giving gays discount at Anfield."

Jimmy rocked back in his seat, "Hah, hah, hah, hah! How much? I might try it myself! …They call it sending in a curved ball, you know."

"Who does?"

"The big guy, probably."

"Have you been at Gran's pills again?"

"Yeah, probably."

* * *

When Jimmy came home from work the following evening, the loft was open with the ladder down, and Molly had her old dress designs spread out over the table.

"Why is the loft open?"

"Sinead's up there, measuring up."

"For what…? I told Terry to keep quiet about that."

"Terry didn't say a word. Why, were you talking about it? Anyway, she had it all worked out by the time Terry got back from the pub. What d'you think of this one?" She showed Jimmy one of her designs. "I did that fifteen years ago. No, hang on a minute, more than that – must have been eighteen years ago. Still good now, though, isn't it? I like that one. Put it in the possibles pile. And we could knock that wall down…" she pointed to the wall to the front parlour. "Sorry, love. How are you? How was your day?"

"You've never asked me how my day was before. But, seeing you've asked, it was alright, thank you… until I got home."

"Good, well put the kettle on. Let's have a cup of tea. We'll have to put an RSJ in. Terry's a joiner, you know."

Jimmy started to walk upstairs.

"Where are you going? Have you put the kettle on? Now, that one can go in the maybe pile... or should it be in the worth-a-second-look pile?"

Jimmy climbed the loft ladder and looked in.

"Hiya, Dad! Look, this is going to be fantastic. There's so much room. Come up and I'll show you what I'm thinking of doing."

The anger, or whatever it was, about not being consulted on any of this, drifted off through the roof as he saw the excitement and delight on his daughter's face. Twenty minutes later he was climbing back down the ladder carrying a box with his wood carvings in.

"She's a bit excited, isn't she! I haven't had time to do any dinner. Could you be a love and go down the chippy." Molly went to her bag, took out some money, and handed it to Jimmy. "Oh, they're your wood carvings. They were good, weren't they – I liked that one."

What about this one? And this one?

"There's just the four of us. JJ's having his tea at Michael's – it's his birthday. Put that box in the corner out of the way. Nobody'll touch it there. There should be enough for a pint, but don't be long. We need to decide what we're going to get JJ for his birthday on Saturday."

Jimmy had enough for three pints. Medicinal purposes.

* * *

The following lunch time at work, "So the wedding's definitely on then?"

"Yeah, you could say that. I'll tell you, Billy, it's no wonder you think I'm going mad. The whole world's gone mad, I think. I come to work these days for a bit of peace – it's supposed to be the other way around, isn't it? And it's JJ's birthday on Saturday, and there's going to be ten kids running round the house."

"He's a ten year old kid, Jimmy. Of course he's going to want a party! Are you going to be giving him that rod of Terry's?"

"No, Terry and Sinead are going to give him that – which you can't blame them for that. They'll need to save up all the money they can. No, we're apparently giving him a Game Boy, or something – a computer game."

"Yeah, I've seen them. Super Mario."

"Well, that's another thing. Super Mario, an Italian plumber. What does he do? Go round saving the world by mending burst pipes? What happened to Superman and Batman – real heroes? And what's the other thing – turtles coming up out of the sewer. Super Ninja Hero Turtles… with names like Donatello – another Italian. Who thinks this stuff up?"

"So, what's happening about the loft?"

"Well, that's going ahead and all. We were all talking quietly, weren't we, the night before last. By the time I got home from work yesterday, Sinead was working out how to get flat pack furniture through the hole in the ceiling! But it had nothing to do with Terry. I'm glad about that. Apparently, by the time we got back from the pub Sinead had it all worked out. Anyway, I'm going round to Terry's mate's house next Friday to see the job he's done on his loft."

* * *

The birthday went off without any major incidents, which means there were no ambulances. Sunday morning, Jimmy expected to be dragged out of bed to go fishing, but he had no idea where. He thought of trying the lake, but somebody had told him you've got to have a permit. *I'm not getting a bloody permit*, he thought, *it's going to be a seven-day wonder*. But he needn't have worried;

the big hit of JJ's birthday was the Game Boy. It came as some relief; he could have a lie-in, but by eleven o'clock he wished he had gone fishing as it was becoming clear this wasn't the house he knew any more. It had become the headquarters of strategic planning. Jimmy took refuge in the yard. He got his old Black and Decker Workmate out of the shed and proceeded to get lost in a lump of spalted beech, and that's where all his spare time went over the next few days, apart from mealtimes which were mostly with a tray on the knee, watching telly, which was actually the norm – but now there was no choice because what they used to call their dining table had been commandeered and was now a sewing table. Overnight, lists appeared, pinned to the wall at various appropriate places, and as the days went on they grew in number and length. The conversation around the house changed from "I don't care, you're not bringing that in here," and, "Where have you been till now?" to, "I don't see why we should invite her when we weren't invited to her anniversary party, when practically the whole street was…" and, "How about inviting one or two of your teachers? Give the do a bit of class. That'll be one in the eye for our Celia."

Celia was Molly's older sister. They didn't see each other very often, apart from on occasions such as this. She lived in Childwall, in a detached house, with all the bits that went with it, including husband – Brian, an accountant.

"She hasn't even been round to see how her own mother is settling in."

* * *

The next Friday in the Duck House:

"I tell you, Billy, the house has been taken over by the female mafia, and I'm at the bottom of the pecking order. My function in the scheme of things is to go to the chippy – oh, and book the cars."

"Well, it's a wedding, Jimmy, what the hell do you expect? Have they named the date?"

"Oh, yeah. Six weeks tomorrow."

"Six weeks! And it's a church do?"

"Oh, yeah."

"How the hell has she managed to book a church for six weeks' time, and on a Saturday?"

"Don't know. Must have had a cancellation. Or Daisy's put a horse's head in someone's bed."

"That'll be it."

"And Molly's making the dresses, would you believe. There's patterns and bits of cloth all over the place. I go to sit down and somebody shouts 'Hang on a minute – let's move that first'."

Billy chuckled, "You've got my sympathy, buddy. They're squeezing eighteen months of intensity into six weeks!"

"Why, though, mate? It just makes it so hard. Why don't they just go to a register office like we did?"

"Well, you're wasting your time, aren't you, you can't take on the mafia. Have you booked the cars?"

"No, if I phone the cars they'll tell me to phone back the day before I need them. But they don't want those cars, do they, they want the black shiny ones driven by a suit and cost ten times the price."

"Who's paying for all this? Where's all the money coming from?"

"Daisy, isn't it. She's apparently sitting on a bit of a nest egg. Which is decent of her. Oh, and Daisy's making the cake, the wedding cake."

"What, with eye of toad and tail of newt?"

"Yeah, I wouldn't touch it if I was you. Which reminds me: I've been told to tell you you're invited. You'll get an official one, I suppose – and bring your buddy, Dimitri."

"No, no! He won't want to come."

"Hey! Don't ask him – tell him! I'm going to need all the back up I can get. Half of Molly's side are from Childwall."

"Yeah, OK then, I'll tell him you need back up. Where's the reception?"

"Good question. There's a short-list of three. I'm not getting involved. So, do us a favour, make sure you bring Dimitri. If you don't, I'll get the blame. But keep quiet, because if JJ knows Dimitri's coming he might try and get him to bring that young lad, Janni."

"No, he won't do that!"

"No, you're probably right, but just in case – I don't need any more hassle."

"Did you go and see that loft job, by the way?"

"Oh, don't ask!" Jimmy went to the bar to get some more beer.

"So?" said Billy, when Jimmy came back, "What was the loft like? Is it no good?"

"No, it's brilliant! He's done a fantastic job. But that's another thing – the loft's got to be done in six weeks. It does look tidy, though. There are some good tradesmen about, aren't there. D'you ever regret packing in the Army? You had a good job there, didn't you."

"No, had enough after five years."

"The shit in the Middle East?"

"No, the shit's everywhere. It was the shit below the surface I couldn't be doing with. The Army's alright if you don't ask too many questions. Or, if you do, don't expect a straight answer. Still, I got a decent trade out of it, I suppose."

"Oh, of course, sparking. You know how the electricity runs along the cable."

"I suppose so. I was attached to the communications – or, should I say, the lack of it. It's all politics. Whatever strings Washington pull, Whitehall jumps to it. No, the fork-lift truck'll do me for now."

***

Jimmy didn't sleep well that night; in fact he hadn't for the last few nights. It wasn't just the wedding. Under normal circumstances he would have taken that in his stride, but these weren't normal circumstances, so he couldn't. He kept getting flashes of the Wilderness.

Saturday morning, Jimmy was in the back yard with his Black and Decker Workmate and spalted beech.

How or why the idea came to him was difficult to know. Was it forged by some unseen force? Doesn't really matter; it was there. If he drilled a hole at an angle in the wood and fitted a piece of bamboo cane, about three feet long, into the hole so it stuck up like the jib of a crane, he could then suspend another, horizontal, piece of bamboo from the top of the jib to make a set of scales. Then he could hang a houseplant on one side, counterbalanced with some pebbles on the other... *That would be quite effective. No – very.*

While he was pondering the work involved, for instance the lump of wood had to look right: not flat and square, not at all. Quite the opposite. But right. Which meant removing quite a bit of its weight, but then the weight was actually essential to stop the crane overbalancing.

Despite his absorption in the project, every now and then his mind snapped back to the Wilderness, like an unexpected split appearing in the wood that wouldn't go away until it was dealt with. He found himself calling out in a loud whisper, "Voice! ...Voicie! ...I need to talk."

"Fire away, Jimmy boy."

"Oh! You're there. It's just I need to talk. What you said in the Wilderness – the disciple thing…"

Molly came out into the yard looking around. "Who are you talking to?"

"Oh, me? The wood. You've got to talk to it, tell it you love it."

"Well, keep it down. Sinead and Terry have got to go round to the church to see the priest and they're practising what they've got to say. She's had a feeling he may not be happy about her being," she whispered, "pregnant," and mimed a bump on her stomach.

"Well, get your mam on the case."

"I know. That's next."

"OK, well I'm going for a walk down the park," he said a bit slowly and deliberately so Voice could hear him. "I'll be able to talk to my wood there!"

"OK. Well, go out the back way."

Jimmy went in the house to reassure his daughter and told her the priest was probably just going to make sure they understood the commitment and the importance of the marriage vows. Then he shouted to Molly.

"I'll go out the front."

"What about your lump of wood?"

Jimmy hesitated. "I've got a small piece in me pocket."

"OK, so long as you've got a small piece in your pocket."

* * *

As Jimmy walked down towards the park he passed the skip in Acacia Street.

"Hiya, Jimmy, I see what you mean."

"What? Is that you, Voice?"

"Yes, of course. I see what you mean – the stuff people throw out."

"Are you in the skip?"

"Too right!"

"Well, come on. We've got to get to the park. What are you doing in the skip?"

"Came to see the bath, and got a bit carried away. Not very often I get a chance to mooch about in stuff like this. What's this for? Hang on a moment, there's two of them."

"Voicie – park – Wilderness. Remember?"

"Wilderness, park. You're right. I'll catch up with you in practically no time. Well, in actually no time."

Jimmy walked on towards the park, as Voicie whispered to himself, "Gordon Bennett! Look at this. Could have used one of them a thousand years ago… Mind you, probably wasn't invented then."

Jimmy was leaning on the railings, looking at the lake.

"OK, mate. Fire away. It's the wedding, isn't it."

"Well, yeah, partly – but it's all the other stuff as well."

"What like? Oh, you mean the Disciple bit?"

"You did say that then? I wasn't dreaming it?"

"Oh no. Big thing that. You should be proud of it. The Big Guy has high hopes in that department – but that's long term."

"And the Wilderness? What's all that about?"

"I'm glad you mentioned that. Got a bit of a bollocking for not taking that seriously enough. In a Godly way, you understand." Voice paused for a moment, "Look, got an idea. Let's just run this by you. How about…," he hesitated, "How about me and you go back to the Wilderness – just thinking out loud, mind – go back to the Wilderness till the wedding. You get out of the house and all the hassle, and we've got a chance to talk, bounce a few ideas around, that sort of stuff. How about that?"

"Oh, yeah, that'll be great."

"Good. See you Monday."

"Hang on. I was being sarcastic. I thought you were joking."

"No, no. Serious. See you Monday."

"Hang on a minute. What about Molly, and work?"

"They won't miss you. I told you that. So, if that's all, I'll scoot. I want to get back to the skip while I've still got a few moments left."

Jimmy walked on, put his hands in his pockets, and pulled out a little piece of wood. "Did you hear all that?" As he wandered round the lake, then back home, he felt a lot more relaxed, smiling as he passed people. He told himself it was because he'd talked with Voice. Always better to clear the air. But it was more than that, and deep down he knew it was. On Monday he was going back to the Wilderness but, instead of the thought filling him with unease and trepidation about the impending isolation, he felt a warm glow, a tingling feeling that didn't make sense. *It's the thought of being away from the wedding mania – that'll be it.* He passed the skip without a second glance.

The house, too, was relaxed and peaceful. Sinead had got back from the church; Jimmy had been right. She and Molly were at the table playing wedding dresses.

"Did you have a good chat with your wood?"

"Yep." Jimmy carried on to the back yard, not to hide, but to get back to his work. A few minutes later, Molly brought him a cup of tea.

"Look at this, Moll. It's going to be like scales. I'm going to put a plant – you know, a house plant – on one side and pebbles on the other, and the plant's going to rise up as it dries out so it'll tell you when the plant needs watering."

"Oh, what a good idea!"

He had said it without thinking; it was a good idea, but where did it come from?

* * *

The following Sunday, Jimmy took JJ to the park. Molly and Sinead had gone to Cheshire Oaks near Ellesmere Port, one of those massive retail parks that had sprung up over the last few years. Jimmy and Daisy despised them. Were they the only ones who knew that they had been invented for the sole purpose of extracting every penny from innocent people? And, despite their outrageous claims of half price/massive discounts, giving very little in return when you consider the built-in redundancy of all the stuff people were buying, and the little difference it was going to make to their wellbeing anyway.

Jimmy and JJ sat on the grass watching the lake stretch out in front of them. JJ hadn't really talked much about the fishing lately; since his birthday his Game Boy had pulled rank. Jimmy had watched his son grow into a little man in Corfu and now he had melted back into the ten year old boy again.

"It was a good holiday, wasn't it lad, Corfu?" They both stared across the water, each drifting into their own memories.

"Yeah, it was."

"Fishing wouldn't be quite the same here, would it."

"No, it wouldn't."

"But the fishing was good in Corfu, wasn't it lad."

JJ looked up at his dad, beaming, "It was, wasn't it, Dad."

"It was. And those two fish you caught on the last day… and they cooked it up for us, didn't they. What was that place called?"

"It was the Acropoly, Dad."

"And everybody had some, didn't they."

JJ's heart filled with pride as he again saw Dimitri carrying the silver platter.

"So, even if you don't get to use your fishing rod very often, it's going to remind you about that night, isn't it? And so will this," he took the penknife out of his pocket. "Did you forget about this?"

"No, Dad, I didn't forget. I knew you had it."

"I think perhaps I should hang on to it a bit longer if you don't mind."

"You will look after it, though, won't you?"

"Cheeky sod!" Jimmy pushed him over.

JJ got up and dived on his dad's back, and they wrestled around on the grass.

When they got back home, Daisy was bringing a steak and kidney pie out of the oven. She cleared the table, and twenty minutes later the three were eating pie, chips and beans, with bread and butter so they could make chip butties. Food could not get any better.

Chapter 17

Despite a good night's sleep, Jimmy woke up on Monday morning with some trepidation – not about his imminent adventure, not as such, but how was it going to work? He still couldn't come to terms, despite the assurances from Voice, with the thought that he would not be missed. To start with, it was his turn to drive to work, pick up Billy outside the paper shop, and if there was time a quick cup of tea before they started…

"Sorry, don't do tea," said Voice.

….Jimmy looked round at the strangely familiar surroundings.

"I've checked you in," said Voice. "Mr Efficiency today. That's your cave, over there."

Jimmy looked around again, wondering where the cave was. His eyes focused on what appeared to be an opening in the rock.

"Yes, that's the one, Jim."

Jimmy walked over slowly and looked in.

"Don't worry, the bear's probably asleep."

"What?" said Jimmy as he quickly retreated.

Voice laughed. "No bear – just a joke. Just a little celestial brevity to welcome you… help you relax."

"Help me relax, putting a bear in me cave?"

"Oh, see what you mean. Take your point. No more bear jokes. You haven't asked me how I managed to swing six weeks in the Wilderness at such short notice. Wasn't easy you know," said Voice, anxious to reclaim the higher ground.

"Oh, sorry Voice. I had no idea. How did you pull it off?"

"Well, actually, I told them in a manner of speaking most people spend all their lives in the Wilderness and some never come out of it."

"That's quite clever!"

"Yes, I thought that. I actually entered it for Profound Observation of the Week."

"What?"

"Oh yeah, we have those sort of things. Profound Observation of the Week, Best Hairstyle of the Week, Best Funny of the Week – you won that one."

"What?"

"You know, when you first went into the airport, and I said you were the Disciple, and you thought I said trifle… That was so funny, you went straight to Number One."

Jimmy's mind flashed back and he recalled telling Billy that a voice had called him a trifle, and became acutely embarrassed, and hurt at being laughed at.

"Oh, don't get upset, bud. You became a star. Trifle became number one pud in the staff canteen. It probably still is now – it's called a Jimmy Downie. You were number one funny for nearly a week… until someone posted on some extra-terrestrial website a picture of Osama Bin Laden, with a todger like a tree trunk. Apparently someone photographed him somewhere in the Greek islands. But I'm afraid my Profound Observation didn't get anywhere; apparently someone else had already said it."

"But it got me here, though, didn't it."

"Oh yes, it did that… that and a cancellation."

And so, eventually, the first of Jimmy Downie's forty days in the Wilderness came to an end.

He went into his cave. He spread some straw out for his

bed, and lay down. His feet snuggled into something warm and furry, and there he fell into a deep and peaceful sleep. When he awoke in the morning, the bear had already left, muttering something about "one not being able to call one's cave one's own any more."

* * *

"Morning, Jim. Sleep well?"

"Yeah, I did actually. Thought I heard something about an hour ago, but no – yeah, slept very well."

"Warm enough?"

"Yeah, my feet were as warm as toast."

"Right. Well, what are we going to do today?"

"I'm hungry. Did I hear you say something about a staff canteen?"

"Yeah. Not here, though. That's in H. But the food's crap anyway. They brought this new chef in about two hundred and fifty years ago with his poncey ideas. I'd rather have good old traditional food like the steak pie and chips you had on Sunday."

"Oh, shurrup! I'm starving."

"Well, there's that chicken over there."

Jimmy looked around and, sure enough, there was a chicken standing on a boulder a few yards away. "What am I going to do with that?"

"Well, eat it."

"Can't eat it. It's not cooked. Not even dead."

"OK, then. Forget food. Let's get to work. Why are you here? What do you expect to get out of it? I've got one of those bloody multi-choice things: (a) be more tolerant of my fellow man; and (b) don't be so quick to judge other people."

"I can't do this!"

"I totally agree – those two questions mean the same thing."

"No. I mean, yes they do, but I'm hungry. I need to eat something."

"Chicken?"

Jimmy had seen chickens before, of course he had, but they came in two categories: the ones that scurried around the farmyard; and the ones that lay motionless in the supermarket, bald, pink, minus head and feet, and quite, quite dead.

"I don't think you're going to have a lot of choice."

Jimmy looked around, and around. There were rocks. Small rocks, big rocks, and bigger rocks, gravel and dust, the odd petrified tree… and the chicken. Jimmy sat down on a rock, depressed. He hadn't thought about food. If he had, he would have brought a Mars bar or something, but that wouldn't last six weeks.

I'll just sit here and starve to death.

After about ten minutes, he hadn't died and he was still hungry.

"What's the percentage of people who starve to death in the Wilderness?"

"Don't know, but I imagine it to be pretty low. I mean, it wouldn't be good for business, would it? I mean, people are supposed to come here to find themselves, not lose themselves."

"I could kill for a Mars bar."

"Well, kill the chicken."

Now, if somebody had made a video of the next hour and a half it would definitely have gone into the Top Five Videos of the Week, maybe even made number one. But they didn't.

Jimmy first of all sneaked up on the chicken in a somewhat clumsy way, in order to give chicken a fighting chance. Chicken, observing the feeble attempt, casually hopped on to a higher boulder, then a branch of a dead tree. This went on for some time before Jimmy realised the chicken was taking the piss. *No more Mr Nice Guy*, he thought: the gloves were off. Which wasn't a particularly good idea, because some of the rocks were pretty rough, and he'd heard that chickens could give a pretty nasty peck when cornered. Another hour and a half later, Jimmy sat back on the same rock, exhausted, and hungrier than ever.

"Try throwing a stone," said Voice.

Jimmy looked at the chicken. It was only a few yards away. *Why not?* Jimmy stretched and yawned in time-honoured tradition in order to lull the chicken into a false sense of security. He picked up a stone about the size of a golf ball and hurled it in the direction of the chicken. He missed by about three feet. Nevertheless, the chicken fell down, dead.

"I thought I missed it?"

"You did. The chicken died of fright."

"Why?" Not that he was really bothered why the chicken was dead. He was on it, plucking away.

An hour later, Jimmy had a fire going, through the two-stick method, and in another hour and a half he was tucking into the finest chicken ever. Now with a full stomach he was feeling on top of the world, or at least on top of the Wilderness.

"Why did the chicken drop dead?"

"It was the shock. Didn't expect that. You sent in a curved ball."

That was the second time he'd heard that phrase recently. He felt a bit sad: he'd tricked the chicken. Didn't seem fair. He recalled the last time he'd heard that phrase; it was when he'd found out that Billy was gay. It had come as a bit of a shock. Didn't expect it. Just like the chicken. He had nothing against gay people, hadn't really thought about it, but now he did. How could he have been so stupid, not knowing? Everybody else seemed to know. Billy was no different, he was still the same lad.

Jimmy wandered around the Wilderness, just a bit, making sure he didn't lose sight of his cave. There were no roads, no maps, no landmarks. Well, not the usual ones like pubs, traffic lights and shops. Perhaps Billy had changed a bit, he thought. He did seem happier… more talkative, more confident. *For all these years*, he thought, *I'd assumed he was like me, you know, normal.*

The next morning Jimmy woke up having again had a good night's sleep, although his feet were cold. He reflected on his thoughts of yesterday. How many more people did he know that weren't normal? He thought of the various people he knew in the Duck House and at work, and his neighbours. One by one he discounted them, and eventually came to the conclusion he was the only one that was normal – which was sufficient to satisfy him for the moment. There was still plenty of chicken left, so food wasn't a problem, *though it will be tomorrow*, he thought. *I expect another chicken will turn up. God will provide. God? Is there a god?*

"Voicie?"

"Yes, Jim."

"Er, not quite sure how to put this… er, never been big on religion…"

"Well, yeah, I know. That had a lot to do with you being chosen."

"Well, that's another thing. I'm not really sure I'm the right guy for the job."

"What job?"

"Well, that's another thing."

"I think we'd better rein back on the other things until we can establish what the first thing is."

"Yeah… Yeah, see your point. Can you give us a minute?"

In order for Jimmy to take time to collect his thoughts, he decided to do some target practice – just in case there was a god and another chicken appeared. He set up a row of six stones, the approximate size of a can of beans, on top of a boulder. He paced back about ten yards, collected some small stones for ammo, the object being to knock the targets off the boulder in turn, each one representing the head of a chicken, because he didn't think he could rely on the element of surprise next time, even though the only chicken to witness yesterday's stone-throwing – the only previous demo – had died in the process.

The minute Jimmy had allocated to thinking time had now stretched to several hours, while he wrestled with the question that had bothered man since the beginning of time: how best to kill a chicken, and was there a god?

As time went by, his aim steadily improved. He was definitely getting closer to the boulder, and on two occasions he nearly hit it, but the six stones on top simulating the head of the only representative of the food chain remained blissfully unaware of any aerial bombardment.

He decided, rather than ask Voice 'are you sure there is a god?' which could be deemed a bit offensive, given the numerous references to date to the aforesaid deity, and indeed his current postcode, to ask Voice 'what does God look like?' which he thought was extremely clever. He wouldn't only get the answer to the age-old question, he would also get the answer to the second ageist-oldest. What he did overlook, however, was that Voice could, and did, read his thoughts.

"An interesting question, Jimmy. Don't know. Never seen Him. Which raises another interesting question: how do we know He is a him, and not a her, She? And this seems to be a day for interesting questions. Why do we not have a word to indicate the single person without having to state gender? We have them, those and they, all stating a number of people that could be one gender or another, or a mix of; and yet we don't have a word for the single person that can do the same.

"And now that leads on to yet another one. I expect you're going to ask me, if I haven't seen God – don't even know whether 'it' is a man or a woman – how do I know there is one?"

"Well, no. Actually, I was going to ask you if you wouldn't mind if I had a piece of chicken while we kick the ball around. But that was definitely going to be my second question." Jimmy got a piece of chicken, which was now leaving little more than a few bits and the carcass.

"Well, it's a question of belief. Up in H we cover a number of religions. Some have different ideas of what, or who, God is. Some believe that there isn't one god; just a supreme guidance, a force that cannot be compared to any human form at all, but fundamentally they all amount to the same thing: the difference between good and evil, right and wrong, and an unquestionable belief that there is a bigger picture. Sorry, Jim, if I went a bit serious there. Well, I need to sometimes. It's big stuff. But belief is the key, and you can't teach that. Neither can you impose it: that'll never work in the long term. That's got to be down to the individual."

Voice could see he was losing his audience. Jimmy's mind was revolving around chicken, and the remains on the skeleton, and what would Molly do with it… and what's Molly doing anyway?

"It's a bit like Liverpool, isn't it."

Jimmy's ears pricked up. "What?"

"Well, you can't tell anybody to be a passionate Liverpool supporter, can you. You've got to feel it in the gut, haven't you, and then it goes straight to the heart."

"Hey, you're alright, you, Voicie. I've never heard of it that way before, but you're absolutely right. But I've been thinking… you do talk to him, don't you – I mean God – you can talk to him?"

"Of course. Everybody can, though I suppose I have something of a direct line."

"Although you've never seen him," said Jimmy inquisitively, "he still moves in mysterious ways?"

"Absolutely. That's kind of his signature dish."

"Well, I wonder if you could ask him – don't want to sound cheeky, you know, a bit hard-faced, being the new kid on the block and all, or in this case the boulder – whether he could see his way to improving my throwing in the accuracy department should another chicken trundle on to the savannah. That would qualify for a movement in a mysterious way, wouldn't it?"

"Well, I suppose it could, if you hadn't suggested it. You see, one of the key components of the mysterious ways thing is the unexpected, the element of surprise, the mystery. Take all that away, and it becomes 'God moves in totally predictable ways His wonders to perform', and then it's lost some of its bite, some of its va-va-voom, hasn't it."

"I suppose so."

"It's like a magician showing you how he does his trick before he does it…"

"Yeah. Get your point."

"Or knowing the result of the football match before you go to watch it…"

"I get your bloody point, OK?"

"Yes, of course you do. Sorry about that, but life can be a bit of a bitch."

Jimmy wasn't exactly missing Molly, and for some reason he could accept that he wasn't being missed either, but shouldn't he send her a postcard as people do when they're away from home? But none of the usual greetings seemed to fit:

Wish you were here? …*No.*

The weather's wonderful? …*There isn't any.*

With a photo of a beautiful sandy beach, or of the local talent? Or the big fat woman with the little man in a bowler hat? …*But then there isn't a shop to buy the postcards.*

"And there isn't a post box to post them anyway," said Voice, "So don't worry about all that. They're fine. It will all make sense before long… but don't hold your breath," he whispered the last bit to himself.

* * *

The next day, the chicken had been sucked clean some time ago, and the ravenous hunger pains returned.

Bits and pieces of what Voice had been trying to say, and indeed saying, were floating around the air. Some drifted into Jimmy's ear, and then other orifices. Some drifted out again, but some settled down in the deep recesses of Jimmy's subconscious. Was there a god, or something of that ilk? And was Liverpool really the greatest football team ever? Well, Voice was right on the last point, he thought, although Voice didn't actually say that. So he might be right about God.

Jimmy wandered further and further into the Wilderness in search of food, with renewed vigour, renewed hope, with the burgeoning belief that God will provide.

Alas, nothing. Not a sausage – although he didn't really expect to find a sausage. As he grew hungrier and hungrier, he grew weaker and weaker, inevitably coming to the conclusion that the end was nigh. He always knew the end would come one day but, for some reason, he thought he would have some control over it… not like this, surely not like this, in the Wilderness; no opportunity to say his last farewells to his loved ones. Even Voice was unable to offer a little comfort.

Then, in the best Hollywood tradition, a chicken appeared, strutting along like a catwalk model. She hopped on to a boulder, and there she stood – proud and plump. Jimmy felt a surge of adrenaline. *I've got one chance to kill it stone dead, or it'll be away.* The chicken stood there, tall, erect, defiant – daring Jimmy to do his worst. He fixed the bird with a steely glare, like the lone gunman in the closing scene of High Noon, or Stevie G about to take the penalty that will secure victory in the final of the Champions' League.

There's one thing about the Wilderness that's not generally known, and there's no reason why it should be, really: things, some things anyway, are reversed, the exact opposite of what they used to be. For example, left-handed people become right-handed, and *vice versa*. Generally that is of little consequence, and often goes unnoticed. For instance, as we have previously established, there's no need or facility to send postcards home, and no cupboards or drawers to open, no door knobs, no hand-shaking as such.

Now, whether it was Jimmy's idea to try launching his missile with his left hand, or whether that was suggested by Voice, doesn't really matter. Nevertheless, it provoked some argument. Jimmy maintained it was divine inspiration, and Voice said he'd suggested it. The argument was really a bit stupid, as it amounted to pretty much the same thing, but those kinds of unnecessary disagreements can happen in times of extreme stress and exhaustion. Nevertheless, he opted to launch his missile with his left hand.

Jimmy let fly and the rock flew through the air like a missile – whistled past the chicken's head missing it by no more than half an inch, and hit the bear.

* * *

Everything was quiet and still for a moment, apart from the low rumble that appeared to come from under the ground. Chicken remained proud and defiant, apart from her head which had swivelled one hundred and eighty degrees to look behind her. Jimmy was frozen, mouth open, his eyes fixed on a large brown mound some six feet behind Chicken. It appeared to move, and then it did. As the rumble from underground surfaced, the bear very slowly stood, expanded to his full height, and turned in the direction from which the missile had come. Jimmy and Chicken could have used this time constructively, but they were frozen, petrified with fear. Bear saw Jimmy and Chicken at the same time, and began to growl. The growl that had started underground entered the bear through his feet, travelled up his legs to the pit of his stomach, then into his chest, all the time building in velocity, until it exploded through his jaws. Jimmy and Chicken could do nothing but brace themselves as the full force of the roar hit them. They both leaned towards the roar at an angle of forty-five degrees to avoid being blown over. Jimmy's hair stuck straight out behind him, and his cheeks stretched with the G-force. Chicken held position on the boulder, which is a testament to the focus and determination of the true prima donna at the top of her game. Alas, she was bald; every single feather apart from three or four scrawny ones round her ankles had left and were heading towards the Wilderness next door.

Bear took one step forward and scooped Chicken off the boulder, then cleanly bit off her head, by way of an *amuse bouche*, accompanied by a pitiful yell from Jimmy who was now crouching, shivering, behind a rock.

Now, with regard to the left becoming right rule, and as with all sweeping generalisations, there is a tendency to throw up bizarre and ridiculous examples. It is pretty widely known that a chicken, once beheaded, can still run around for a minute or two. Well it didn't; it just lay there, motionless. But the bear did, taking on the mantle of the dead chicken. He danced around, well, like a headless chicken, while trying to make some sort of cluck-cluck sound, then crashed into a rock, and fell over, stunned. Well, this was the funniest thing Jimmy had ever seen, and he laughed and laughed, mixed with a bit of hysteria resulting from the cocktail of sheer terror and uncontrollable laughter. This made Jimmy's legs so weak he too fell over. And there he lay, just for a moment or two, until he opened his eyes and found himself lying nose to nose with the bear.

Jimmy was the first to come to his senses, and he ran off at full speed into… God knows where. The bear's first reaction was to tear after him, but his second, and overriding, one was to go and eat the chicken. Jimmy ran and ran, and spent the whole night running, collapsing with exhaustion, getting up, and running again.

It was probably just before dawn when Jimmy's exhaustion took over and he slept for a few minutes. He was awoken when it was light by a voice saying, "Have you heard the phrase 'it's always darkest before the dawn'?" Jimmy, through sleepy eyes, mumbled, "Yes."

"Shit," said Voice, "I can't enter that one, either. Nevertheless, it's true."

As is often the case in these circumstances, Jimmy's maniacal run through the night had brought him full circle back to his familiar home ground. There was no sign of the bear; he'd gone. But there, on his preparation boulder near his campfire, was half of the chicken from the night before.

Bear knew what it was like to go hungry to the point of starvation. He had lived in the Wilderness for many years.

* * *

The general ethos of the Wilderness was one of self-discovery and developing more compassion for one's fellow man, and a deeper understanding of one's path to enlightenment. Although little of this philosophy was designed to apply to bears, there was inevitably a bit of it going to be absorbed by the few animals that wandered about, and not least by Bear. By way of illustration, at the time of the incident Bear was actually meditating, not on this occasion in order to understand the greater meaning of the universe, but to see how best to win the object of his heart's desires and partake in some Holy Mother of God rumpy pumpy. Sassy resided in the Wilderness next door, which was some way away, and to which you may recall Chicken's feathers were now heading. So one has to have some empathy with Bear because at the time the rock hit him on the back of the head he had reached the part in meditation where he was at least guaranteed first base. Then, bang!

Jimmy stared at the half chicken for an age, then gave Voice a sidelong look in the direction from which Voice had last spoken, which was some time ago now.

Voice, understanding the meaning of the sidelong look, said, "I'm over here."

Jimmy switched direction, "What d'you make of this?" he asked, looking at the half chicken.

"Well, personally, I'd make a curry… partly because I haven't had a curry for a while, and partly because…" Voice paused for a moment, deep in thought, "No, there's just one partly. I'd make a curry. But of course that's no help to you. You haven't got the ingredients."

Jimmy looked around hoping for a clue, some sort of indication as to why Bear would leave half the chicken. He looked towards the cave and wondered if Bear was in there.

"You see … you haven't got any cumin, or coriander… or chilli. Do you use fresh chillies or chilli flakes?"

"Shurrup," said Jimmy as he slowly walked towards the cave.

"I sometimes put in coconut milk or peanut butter… or sometimes I put in both."

"Just shut up, will you, and go and have a look in the cave."

"Ah, well, difficulty there, Jim. Tall and short of it, not allowed. Against AA code of practice."

"Alcoholics Anonymous?"

"No, no… archangels… Ah, you knew that. You were having a little joke with Voicie, weren't you."

"Just cut the crap, and go and have a look in the cave, and see if the bear's there."

Voice tried more delaying tactics, but Jimmy wasn't having any. He knew all the tricks from years of watching football.

"Aren't you going to have some chicken? You must be starving. You could have it, er, er… How about smoked chicken? That's very nice, I believe. Yeah, smokin'."

Jimmy still wasn't having any. He wasn't interested in food. He was exhausted, needed to sleep. He covered the chicken with some small stones, made a feeble attempt to tidy up the muck kicked up from the events of the night before. Eventually, they both went nervously to look in the cave. It was empty. With a sigh of blessed relief, Jimmy curled up on the straw and fell fast asleep.

He slept and dreamed, and slept some more. How long? Difficult to say. Not important. Time itself ceased to be important, as if it didn't exist any more. When he eventually woke up, he got up, stretched, and wandered around. Everywhere looked different, although it wasn't. He was just seeing it as though for the first time. Not as a stark, barren landscape, but as a place of… what? …He didn't really know.

The chicken was still there under the pile of stones. *I'll have it later*, he thought. He tidied the cave, made a makeshift brush out of some tumbleweed, and lit a fire just to make it more homely. He sat by the fire and reflected on recent events, which were fast becoming a blur, a distant memory. One thing he'd learned, though: when you think things can't possibly get any worse, they can – and probably will. But then, by some force outside comprehension things work out OK… No, better than OK.

It was some time before Bear returned. He just trundled in, looking tired but with something of a smug, self-satisfied grin. He nodded to Jimmy and went into the cave and slept.

As that cave was the only one in the immediate vicinity, without a great deal of conversation Bear and Jimmy decided to share it. What started off as a marriage of convenience developed. They sometimes had their meal together by the fire, swapping stories, and occasionally Jimmy tucked his feet into the brown fur as he slept.

"I'll tell my grandchildren about Prima Donna," said Bear, as his mind drifted to the Wilderness next door, "...of how she stood there, proud and defiant."

"Who's Prima Donna?"

"Chicken's Prima Donna! You called her Prima Donna!"

"No, I didn't!"

"You must have."

"No, no. Definitely you."

This exchange carried on for some time without being resolved, which is quite common, not just in the Wilderness but in society generally. It didn't develop into a full-blown dispute. In fact, quite the contrary. They became good friends, but it was more than that; it was mutual respect, though chicken never tasted the same again.

Chapter 18

As the days drifted by, Jimmy became more and more at home in the Wilderness. He was surprised at how little he missed the material world, the other world that he knew he would return to one day. He spent many long hours talking with Voice about philosophy and true values, and the point of it all. Being detached from the other world enabled him to see it in clearer perspective. The lust for money that he shared with everybody else seemed so shallow; did it just lead to greed and corruption, and the lack of true satisfaction or fulfilment?

"Well, do something about it," said Voice.

"Oh, yeah, like how?"

Voice remained silent.

"Like how?" he repeated. "How can one person make a difference?"

"One person can't help making a difference. Everything affects everything. Go and put the telly on."

And there, behind him, was a television.

"Plug it in."

"What?"

"Plug it in."

Next to the telly was a cable hanging down with a plug on the end. Jimmy went over and picked it up.

Voice laughed, "Sorry, Jim. No electric here – celestial joke

– but for some reason it seems to work anyway. Get the remote and sit down."

He got the remote, sat down and pressed the button. What came on the screen was the park, the lake, with Jimmy and Billy.

"That's me and Billy!"

"Yes, just watch."

"Is there anyone on Corfu you didn't give one to?"

"Right," said Voice, "See that old couple on the bench? They could hear that. You were in the park for an hour and ten minutes walking round the lake. You passed the old couple three times."

"No wonder the goats were nervous when you were around!"

"Too fucking right!"

The picture stayed with the old couple.

"I wouldn't mind giving it one meself," said the old man.

"Hmmm…" she replied.

A few moments later, the couple walked towards the exit, holding hands.

Their pace quickened as each played through the forthcoming scenario.

Jimmy watched in silence. "Do I really look like that? Do I really behave like that? How could I have known Billy was gay?"

"Don't beat yourself up, Jimmy."

But he was. It was like when you hear your voice on a tape recorder for the first time, only ten times worse.

The television fast-forwarded to a month later.

The old couple were sitting in the doctor's surgery. The man went in to see the doctor alone.

Jimmy's attention switched from self-pity to the television screen.

The old man came out of the surgery a few minutes later, smiling. He nodded to his wife and they left. He'd been to ask the doctor for some Viagra.

The screen went black.

"Well?" said Voice.

Jimmy sat there, looking in the direction of the telly but his mind was elsewhere.

"Well," said Voice again, "What d'you think?"

"I don't look like that, do I?"

"How d'you think you look?"

"Not like that – and I don't talk like that, I don't act like that?" There was a questioning tone in his voice.

Voice didn't answer.

"Put the telly on again."

It showed the inside of Jimmy's house. Sinead was trying on a dress, half-made.

"You're going to look absolutely lovely. Now hang on a minute, let's put a couple of pins in."

"Me dad's glad I'm getting married, isn't he?"

"Keep still while I get this bit, or it won't be straight. Of course he is. You know your dad; he doesn't always show it, but of course he is. Just doesn't like all the fuss."

Jimmy stared at the screen, a tear coming to the corner of his eye.

"Press a button," said Voice.

The screen switched to the inside of the Duck House. Jimmy and Billy were sitting at a table talking about the Lottery.

"The most I've ever won is a tenner," said Jimmy, *"and I've been doing it for years. If I could only get a decent win."*

The screen went black.

"What would you do with a decent win?"

"What?"

"What you do with a decent win? Or, perhaps, what would you call a decent win?"

"A few grand. Give her a decent wedding."

"Is that what she wants? Isn't Sinead going to have a decent wedding anyway? And then what – stop doing the Lottery?

Though a new car would be nice, wouldn't it?" Voice changed the subject: "That was decent of Bear, wasn't it, to give you half his chicken… the kindness of strangers."

* * *

Jimmy decided to build a statue, a sort of monument, to Prima Donna, but with no tools, no wood, no spalted beech, all he had was just twigs, stones, tumbleweed – *but I can make some sort of sculpture thing. Bear would like that.* Though he didn't see much of Bear these days; he was spending more and more time in the Wilderness next door.

Voicie was wrong, he thought, *money's not all that bad. OK, it can cause greed and corruption, and probably most of the problems in the world – that, and religion.* Then he checked himself, better leave religion out of it, and looked around cautiously in case any retribution was heading his way.

"Don't concern yourself about that," said Voice, which startled Jimmy, who thought his thoughts were his own at that moment.

"No, that's partly why you're here. Religion's being used as a front to hide a lot of the evil. But of course you knew that in Corfu."

"I did, didn't I," said Jimmy, feeling a tad pleased with himself.

"And even if it isn't, there's just as much greed and corruption in the churches as the rest of the world. Anyway, I didn't mean to interrupt. You carry on with your thoughts – and I like the idea of that Prima Donna thing."

When Jimmy was reasonably satisfied Voice had gone, as far as he ever went; *all I want is a few thousand – that's hardly greedy.* He collected a bit of tumbleweed and some twigs. But then that was all he'd ever wanted: just a bit more than he had. Like the demented donkey chasing the carrot. He recalled how Harry used to do the football pools every week. There was skill in that, he used to say. All his vast knowledge of football gained over the years was bound to give him the edge, a better chance than most, but he never won.

What's the point of it all, he'd said before he snuffed it. *Why did he have to say that, and why me?*

"Chicken, bloody chicken," moaned Jimmy as he prepared his meal feeling a bit sorry for himself. "I'm fed up with chicken."

"Try some barbecue sauce. I believe that's one of those new-fandango things used these days to spice up a meal." And there, on Jimmy's preparation boulder was a bottle of barbecue sauce.

"What? Where? I wish you'd stop doing that!" Then he noticed the bottle of sauce. "Where the hell did that come from?"

"The supermarket. There's a new Aldi just opened up."

"Aldi? What the hell are you talking about? Where the bloody hell's Aldi?"

"Over there, over that way," said Voice, before he realised there was no point just saying that without being able to point. "You take the slip road by the yak droppings, if you see what I mean."

"Aldi, eh?" said Jimmy with some delight. "How the hell did that happen?" as he plopped a dollop on his chicken and began eating it with relish – the relish on this occasion being…

"Evolution, I suppose. You can't stop evolution. Though a supermarket wouldn't be my first choice."

"What else have they got?"

"Just that, just barbecue sauce. Oh, and apparently suitcases on Sundays. A special. Though why anybody would want suitcases when all the baggage they carry around is in their heads…"

Jimmy returned to his sculpture with renewed vigour. The barbecue sauce had worked like a tonic. Tumbleweed, stones, bits of dead wood… "Money can't buy you love…" he began to sing.

"Ah, that's a biggie."

"Yeah, the Beatles. Were they big in heaven too?"

"No. I mean yes, they were. But I meant love."

Jimmy thought of Molly.

"Yeah, a biggie," Voice repeated.

"Don't let her hear you call her a biggie – she's very sensitive about that sort of stuff."

"No, I mean love itself, you goon… What's that supposed to be? That one, sticking out there."

"Sticking out where? Just piss off, Voice – it's not finished yet."

By the end of the following day the sculpture was beginning to take shape. Unfortunately the shape did little to resemble a chicken.

"Love – that sure is a biggie," said Voice.

"Yeah, I know. You said that yesterday."

"How many times have you been in love, Jimmy?"

"Oh, I've had my share! Don't you run up and down the street worrying about that."

"But how many times have you actually been in love? Love – really in love."

"Oh, just Molly. Molly's the only one who would ever put up with me."

"And are you the only one who would ever put up with Molly?"

"Oh no – there were loads after Molly. I had to put up a fight to get her."

"A bit like Bear."

"Yeah, he's over in the Wilderness next door again, isn't he, the dirty sod!"

"Is someone talking about me?" said Bear as he returned from his extra-curricular activities, "Ah! Look at that – Prima Donna."

"How on earth did you ever get a chicken from that pile of crap?" said Voice, who could now talk to Bear as well.

"It's symbolic – but what would you know about symbolism? Bear's far more sensitive and artistic than you'll ever be."

"It was the symbolism that told you it was Prima Donna, wasn't it, Bear?"

"Yeah, it was, but I haven't a clue what you're talking about."

"You've been to see Sassy again, haven't you, you sly old bear."

"Oh, I love her, Jimmy. She's an amazing Grizzly."

"I thought she was a Brown Bear?"

"Yeah, Brown Bear. She's an amazing Brown Bear. When she hugs you, you stay hugged. Just imagine that."

"Yeah, I'm afraid I can."

"Bear?" said Jimmy in an enquiring tone, not really sure how this was going to go down, "Bear, being a bear and all, how many times have you been in love?"

"Oh, I've had my share! Don't you go running in and out of the cave worrying about that."

"But how many times have you actually been in love – you know, real love?"

"Just once. Sassy."

"That was quick."

"I was expecting the question. I heard you and Voice talking about it earlier on."

"Why? How? Where were you?"

"Hiding behind that rock over there. I heard you talking to someone who I now know was Voicie, but I didn't then. I thought *he's flipped* – and I'm not sharing my cave with a nutter… I mean, would you?"

"Well, no. But I didn't think I'd be sharing with a bear just a short while ago." Jimmy hesitated, "Does that mean you and Sassy will be shacking up?"

"Living in sin, you mean? Well, yeah. Which means, mate, I may have to boot you out in two or three weeks."

"Well, actually, I expect to be moving on myself round about then."

"Oh, good. You'll tidy your room up before you go, won't you?"

"Oh, yeah – I'll miss you, too!"

"Oh, good. I was dreading bringing that up."

* * *

Jimmy reflected on all the people he knew who had money – not that there were that many. But then what constitutes money? His boss in work, Charlie Madden, had money; new car every couple of years, big detached house, conservatory, and the big gravel drive he had Jimmy working on for a week last year – but still worked eight or ten hours a day and moaned when the bills needed paying. Whatever he had, he still wanted more.

That old guy, Billy Gilbert, he thought, *he won fifty thousand on the Lottery. Bought everybody drinks in the Duck House. Doesn't seem to go to the Duck House any more. They say he's become a bit of a tight sod.*

Half the programmes on the telly are quiz programmes with cash prizes, and the news programmes reporting on how much money the big industries and the banks are making, followed by redundancies here, there and everywhere so they can make more. And education: what d'you want to do when you leave school? Make loads of money.

No money here. No car – don't need one. Don't need petrol... There's a decent life here, a bloke might stay. Oh, but, then he recalled, *I'm being kicked out in a couple of weeks. Wonder if I can get a cave of my own?*

"There are some caves coming up, recently converted. Might suit you."

"I wish you'd stop doing that!" shouted Jimmy, "I was just joking."

"Good. So was I. You're not supposed to be enjoying yourself here: it's supposed to be a time of reflection and self-discovery."

"I am reflecting, and I am self-discovering – like the clappers… Then you butt in and scare the living daylights out of me! Can't you warn me when you're coming? Get a cow bell or something, you know, those things goats wear."

"I could go bing-bong like they do in the supermarket."

"No, no. That would be as bad as just turning up."

They were both silent for a few moments, thinking.

"I tell you one thing you could answer for me Voicie. You know in the supermarket when the tannoy comes on and she says 'This is a staff announcement – will the cleaner please go to aisle six,' or, 'This is a staff announcement – will all till-trained staff please go to the check-out.' Why do they say, 'This is a staff announcement'? Does it mean the rest of us aren't supposed to be listening? Because I do. And if they didn't say it do they think anybody who fancies doing a bit of cleaning will go to aisle six?"

"I don't know, Jim. I think that's one of those things that's a mystery to the universe that can never be answered."

Jimmy reflected on some of the kids at school who had 'done well', as they say, and one or two had gone on to make their fortune. *But has it made them happier? How can you tell? It appeared to, or was that just a front? Is anybody ever truly happy or content?*

"Well, perhaps happy is the wrong word," said Voice, "Perhaps content is more what we're looking for, though that's not the right word either."

"Well, it's not money. All the people with money just seem to want more."

"Or they're terrified of losing what they've already got."

"Are you saying that money's just a drug and everybody's hooked?"

"I'm not saying anything. It's up to you to work it out for yourself."

Jimmy went back to work on his symbolic chicken, but he felt tired, sleepy. He sat down, leaning against the boulder, and fell asleep. When he woke up he was looking towards his sculpture, but through sleepy eyes he didn't recognise it. He knew it was Chicken but, no matter how hard he tried to focus, he couldn't make it look like Chicken. He got up and looked again, and there she was, Prima Donna – exactly as Jimmy had left her. She didn't need any more work, she was there all the time; he just needed his eyes to be wide open.

He decided to go for a walk and find Aldi. The sleep had done him a power of good; he felt recharged. *I've been looking in the wrong place. Instead of looking to see if money made people content, I should look at people who are content and find out how they got there.*

The arid landscape of the Wilderness resembled Corfu in parts. He thought of the old man with the donkey and his little brown dog. *He was content. No money there, but then none of the traps that ambitious people fall into either, although he must have put a lot of work into getting his salad garden in such good order.* Jimmy kicked a stone, and a cloud of dust flew up. *A great deal of work.*

And Father Jakovis – he was a good man. You can't become a priest without ambition, or without determination anyway, and that's not for money, not at that level, not being the priest of a village community, anyway.

Does good and contentment go hand in hand? The old man was certainly good. He remembered the salad. *The kindness of strangers.*

Jimmy felt decidedly pleased with himself, having worked all that out without any help from you-know-who, but perhaps he should have listened a bit more carefully to you-know-who. There was a decided bounce in his step as he approached the yak droppings. He slipped and fell, face down. Splat.

He never did get as far as the supermarket. He staggered back, leaving the glow of self-adulation and pride buried in the crap. He occasionally heard the faint tinkle of what sounded like a cow bell, followed by muted laughter.

"Just button it, Voice."

Chapter 19

From time to time when the television appeared, Jimmy watched Molly and the family back home. He hadn't realised how much he loved her until the other day when Voicie brought it home with a bump. *Could it be? Could it possibly be that true love only happens once?*

The loft conversion was well under way. They were fitting a skylight in the roof. That was straightforward enough, but any big furniture had to come through the house and so a big hole had been cut in the ceiling to the loft, and then would be closed up again. They'd ordered a new mattress to go with a second-hand bed they'd got hold of. Terry took the day off when the mattress was to be delivered, but it never arrived. Twice more they made arrangements for it to be delivered, and it never happened. Eventually it did. The shop was apologetic in a way, offering a voucher for a few pounds to be spent in store. As if money, again, was the solution to everything. One time when the mattress was supposed to be delivered, Terry had arranged to go over and see his mother in Birkenhead and tell her about the wedding, but he never got there.

Mistakes can happen, of course, but the idea that it can be compensated for by a few pounds' store credit – one doesn't really equal the other.

Jimmy saw little JJ walking down the street with his mate, hands in pockets, collar up on his blazer, looking at the ground as he walked, deep in conversation about something very important.

Was that me thirty years ago? he thought, *Or was it just yesterday?*

Sinead and Terry up in the loft, sitting on the bed, leaning against the wall, planning how they were going to change the world.

Molly, sitting at the table with a notebook he hadn't seen before, totting up figures on a calculator, focused, concentrating. He hadn't seen that Molly for a long time.

Daisy, sitting in the armchair in the corner, her eyes closed – not asleep – just closed, overseeing all.

Billy was in the park talking to Dimitri on his mobile. Jimmy was losing Billy.

And Jimmy himself. That was the biggest shock of all. Everybody seemed to have purpose and mission, but what was his? Cracking a few jokes down the Duck House, helping Charlie Madden leap from crisis to crisis? Apart from Liverpool on Saturday, Harry was right: what's the point?

Jimmy didn't recognise himself, or perhaps he just didn't want to. *Is that really me?*

"I don't know what you're seeing."

"That," Jimmy said, nodding towards the television, "Is that how people see me?"

"Not necessarily. Don't we all look beyond the superficial when we look at somebody? Don't we all look at what's going on behind the eyes? Isn't that what Father Jakovis saw, and the old man with the donkey? Perhaps you should open your eyes wider and look at yourself, perhaps then you'll find the point."

"What, contentment, like Father Jakovis and the old man?"

"No, no, not contentment. That's the wrong word."

"What is it, then?"

"You tell me when you've found yourself."

"Oh, great! I've got to go and buy a bloody mirror, then, have I?"

"Yeah, or use the one in your head."

* * *

"Are you content, Bear?"

Bear thought for a few moments, "For about three-quarters of an hour, then I'm ready to go again."

Jimmy felt tired, so he went into the cave for a sleep, but he couldn't – there was too much running round his head. He had to get shut of some of it.

Bear was doing one-arm press-ups, but when Jimmy came out he stopped, a bit embarrassed, and pretended he was looking for something on the floor. "Ah, there it is," he said as he picked up a pebble.

"Bear?" said Jimmy. "Bear?" he said again, "Do you, erm…"

Bear was now sitting up.

"Bear?"

Bear's nose was now one inch away from Jimmy's.

"Do you believe in God?"

Bear flopped down again, "Yes, of course."

"You do?"

"Yes, of course. Never used to, mind, or was never sure, but now I am."

"Sassy?"

"Oh, you want to see her, Jimmy. When she hugs…" He stopped himself, remembering he'd already said that. "Do you?"

"I'm beginning to. No, I think I probably do."

"D'you think God is a lady bear or a man bear?"

Their conversation was interrupted by a small green bush that appeared from behind the rocks. They both stared in disbelief as it shuffled nearer and nearer.

"What's that supposed to be?" asked the bush, apparently referring to Jimmy's sculpture.

Jimmy and Bear looked at each other, then back to the bush.

"Well? Hmm?" said the bush.

"Well, actually it's a statue of a good friend of ours: Prima Donna."

"Not very lifelike. My chest is much bigger than that, and my tail feathers are longer than that. Though you have my head right – proud and defiant." With that, a chicken's head popped out of the bush.

"Prima Donna!" gasped Bear and Jimmy.

Prima Donna had made herself a coat out of little green leaves to cover up her baldness. The three gathered round the campfire to hear Prima Donna's story, Jimmy on his favourite comfy boulder, Bear sitting on the ground, his legs straight out, and Prima Donna perched on the preparation table, not this time as a subject for dinner, but as the prima donna she was and that was her stage. If there were lights at this moment, they would have dimmed, so let's just pretend there were. She waited for her audience to stop fidgeting then, turning herself side-on to her audience, her best side of course, puffed up her chest, extended her head to its full height, then after a long pause began.

"It all began two thousand years ago in the ancient land of the Pharaohs. Queen Cleopatra, contrary to modern myth, was a cat. Not the painted floosie as portrayed by Elizabeth Taylor, for instance.

"Well, one day, while Cleopatra, who at this stage was Princess Cleopatra, was wandering round the Hanging Gardens of Babylon feeling sad and a little melancholic, for she was about to be married to the King of Persia who, though not without good looks, was quite a bit older than her, and, although not entirely without charm and wit, he was heading in that direction. In short, she didn't love him.

"Her mood was interrupted... she looked across to where a voice was coming from, and there, perched on the leg part of a nearby Sphynx, was the most magnificent-looking cockerel. He happened to be the leading actor with a troupe of strolling Shakespearean players."

Prime Donna realised immediately she'd made a big mistake in the historical date thing and hastily said, "This was the Egyptian Shakespeare, which happened about fifteen hundred years before the Hathaway cottage one." She needn't have worried; her audience was gripped, hanging on her every word.

She unbuttoned her green coat and let it swing like a cloak as she strutted from one end of her stage to the other, her bald breast now covered with a down of baby feathers.

"The strolling player's name was George, which she immediately changed to Antony, which was more appropriate.

"Antony and Cleopatra fell madly in love, which was pretty much the only sort available in those days."

Every now and then Prima Donna paused as if for an emotional breather, but really it was to maximise the dramatic effect, and to give a sidelong glance to make sure she had her audience in the palm of her hands.

"They became lovers, but it had to be in secret for in those days royal marriages were a sort of bargaining tool between nations. Something like you show me yours and I'll show you mine.

"So she married the King of Persia, but the marriage was never constipated, but that was kept secret for she actually had ten children: five that looked like a cat but clucked like a chicken; and five that looked like a chicken but miaowed like a cat. But of course that would never do, so they were all disposed of – put in baskets in the bulrushes and sent down the Nile, which caused considerable confusion when somebody else also put Moses in a basket in the bulrushes in the Nile, but that's another story.

"As things came to pass, one of the chicken babies happened to survive, and went on to learn to cluck like a chicken, but part of the cat's DNA has been carried down the line to this day.

"Now who," she addressed her audience, "Now who can tell me who that was?"

Jimmy and Bear remained silent, thinking this was part of her narration.

"I'm talking to you two, cloth ears! Who can tell me who that is?"

Silence.

Jimmy knew, or he'd heard of DNA, but couldn't think what it meant in this case. Bear had totally lost the question.

"What are cats known for?" screamed Prima Donna.

"Oh! Crapping in next door's veg patch," said Jimmie.

"Oh! Scratching the sofa," said Bear.

"Yes, yes! You're both right, but what else?"

"Cats have nine lives?" said Jimmy.

"Exactly!" said Prima Donna with much relief. "Nine lives, which is a bit of an exaggeration – it's more like four or five, and incidentally you two wasted one of them."

Jimmy and Bear looked at the ground, ashamed.

"Well that's in the past now." Prima Donna turned to show

her best side, puffed out her chest and, after a dramatic pause, announced, "I... I am a direct descendent of Cleopatra." She let her audience stay silent for a moment, then said, "I will now take a short break," putting her wing up to her forehead.

"Well, what d'you think of that, Bear?" said Jimmy.

"I know. Fancy her crapping in next door's veg patch!"

"No! I don't mean that: her having nine lives and all – well actually four or five, and, thanks to us, three or four."

When the second act was ready to start, they were feeling decidedly guilty, what with having eaten one of her lives.

Prima Donna noticed this and knew, from a lifetime of experience, you don't – you must not – let your audience feel guilty. "I must say," she stated, "I have come across a great many bears in my time, but none as fierce or ferocious as you, Bear." She knew that was just about the biggest compliment you can give a bear.

Bear beamed with pride and turned to Jimmy, "I am, actually. She's right, you know. I am quite the ferocious one. I'm well known for it."

She went on further at some length, but eventually came to the time when the dirty deed was done. "What I would normally have done in those circumstances," is to pull my head right down into my chest and produce a carrot from under my wing, carved in the shape of a chicken head, and stuck that up. Bear would have snatched and eaten that, and by the time he'd realised he was eating a carrot and not chicken I'd be away, but because of the left-right thing – and Bear's ferocity," she quickly added, "- I forgot which side the carrot was and tragically... Well, the rest you know."

Jimmy and Bear wanted to ask what happened next, but it didn't seem appropriate. Prima Donna bowed and hopped off the stage, looking tired and drained.

Bear remembered something important, and headed off to the Wilderness next door.

Jimmy poked about at the fire a bit, then went for a walk. He saw Prima Donna pecking away at the remains of a carrot. She looked sad. He decided not to invade her space.

* * *

The next day, "Was Prima Donna's story true, Voice?"

"No. Not entirely. Prima Donna's great great grandmother was a cat, and did quite a lot of television work, adverts mostly. She was doing an ad for some air freshener about seven or eight years ago, when she wandered outside for a bit of real fresh air. She'd been cosseted all her life, the finest of everything, apart from life itself. Life itself was a kind of incubator, a goldfish bowl, isolated from anything that the real world had to offer. A young cockerel happened by, and that was it. They rogered each other senseless for two and three-quarter hours, and, well, that was that. So, essentially her story was right, but it wasn't in ancient Egypt; it was in the car park of the Holiday Inn, Milton Keynes. But don't blame Prima Donna for a little bit of dramatic licence. Everybody has a story full of pain and glory. The trick is to see the person inside."

"But how did she get here?"

"What, from Milton Keynes? Well, Milton Keynes is quite close, actually."

* * *

Chicken hopped and strutted around Corfu, for that was the name Jimmy had now given their little area of the Wilderness, partly because of its resemblance to Corfu in places, but in the main as a distraction to give himself something else to think about. Mealtimes were always with or without barbecue sauce, but in his imagination he would prepare a different Greek dish every day. Today was going to be chicken kleftiko.

He wanted to invite Prima Donna, and Bear of course if he was about, but how could he invite Prima Donna to a meal of chicken, no matter how it was disguised?

He couldn't help wondering why she had come up with such an elaborate story. Voice had said it was the theatre in her: born to perform; born to elaborate and thrill and captivate her audience. But Jimmy felt there was more to it than that, for whenever Jimmy saw her on her own she was always quite thoughtful, then when she realised she was being watched she immediately switched to Prima Donna the performer. She was hiding something.

He decided to invite her to dinner.

"Chicken," said Jimmy apprehensively. "It's… kleftiko… only I'm not quite sure whether you'll like it… it's, er…"

"Chicken, you mean?" said Chicken. "No, thank you, but don't get me wrong. You and Bear can eat all the chicken you want, providing you stick with the plebs and leave the aristocracy. She threw back her head and puffed up her chest to remind Jimmy of her breeding, "But I will not eat pleb – no matter how Greek it is. And neither would you if you saw what they ate – they're disgusting." But then, seeing the disappointment on Jimmy's face, she took out a carrot from under her wing and put it on the preparation table, "Though I wouldn't mind if you have carrot."

Jimmy was just about to say, "No, I'm sorry," when he saw a carrot on his preparation table, "Yes, I can do carrot. I do a very nice carrot kleftiko."

"Good. I'll see you about eight o'clock then," and strutted off.

* * *

She arrived twenty minutes late, as was the fashion. Jimmy had decided to give the whole evening a Greek feel, *à la Wilderness*, with chicken kleftiko – or carrot kleftiko as the vegetarian option – and carrot (or chicken) baklava to finish. He thought about improvising some Greek dancing, but decided against it, not really sure whether him dancing arm in arm with Bear might stretch their bonding relationship somewhat. A bottle of wine appeared, courtesy of Voice, which was apparently left over from a recent staff party at Aldi.

The evening was a great success. Chicken had never had Greek food before, which enabled Jimmy to get away with a good deal of artistic licence, though his attempt at pleb baklava was pushing it a tad. So Prima Donna and Jimmy shared the carrot version. It would be wrong to suggest the bottle of wine kept filling itself by way of a minor miracle. Nevertheless, as the evening drew on into the early hours there was more than sufficient to create an evening of much merriment, and occasional deep discussions on life, love, and the point of it all.

It transpired that Prima Donna had had many lovers, which is consistent with chicken society, and especially within the aristocracy. Being part cat, etc., certainly put Prima Donna into that category. Antony was the only one she had ever truly loved, but alas that was not meant to be. Prima Donna didn't need much encouragement from Jimmy to tell the whole story.

Antony was an actor, a poet with a band of travelling troubadours. He wrote her poetry that went straight to her heart and never left it. But he was a dreamer, a romantic, wanted to change the world. He wanted them to go to France and live in a small house on the banks of the Seine, but that was…

"I mean, I can't cluck French," she said.

So they parted, although they never really did.

There was a lot of similarity between the true story and the one she had told a few days ago. Any differences there were didn't really matter.

"You may meet him again," said Jimmy, surprising himself

at becoming sentimental over a soppy story that took place in the car park at Milton Keynes.

"Oh, I know I will. If not in this life, in the next."

"Oh, you believe in heaven, then?"

"Heaven? Oh, you mean Free Range. Of course – that's the only thing that makes sense."

"Swans stay together for life," said Jimmy, trying to impress Prima Donna with the little bit of wild life stuff he knew.

"Don't get me started on swans! They swan around as if they own the place. They're hybrids you know... part duck, part giraffe."

"What?"

"Didn't you know that? Dear me! They were actually the first. That's where the word came from – hybrid. From the latin *hyus bridicust*. It's when a biggie rocks the Casbah with a littlie, the blessing of that liaison is the hybrid."

"Good Lord! That's amazing. I never knew that!"

"Yes, it is. I've got the video somewhere if you want to borrow it. I don't know whether it's been put on DVD yet. I know Attenborough's been after it for years."

Bear listened intently to all this, for, although he was the biggest by a considerable distance, he was the youngest by a considerable distance as well.

Eventually tiredness crept over our little band of three, and so to bed…

* * *

And Jimmy slept and Jimmy dreamed
And dreamt of many things
Of kings and queens and Milton Keynes
And bumble bees with stings

Chapter 20

It was about midday before Jimmy woke up. He went outside and there was an egg, a parting gift from Prima Donna. But as Jimmy went to pick it up, so Bear arrived with exactly the same idea. They stopped and stared at each other, each one believing the tasty morsel was theirs. Bear had spent the rest of the night in the Wilderness next door, engaged in... well, let's just say his hunger was now in the food department. But Jimmy knew it was a gift left by his dinner guest.

Bear rose to his full height, and a roar began to rumble from the deep, but Jimmy's mind was elsewhere. He walked over, picked up the egg and handed it to Bear.

"You have the egg, Bear. I think it's time I went home," and walked on. "Look after Sassy," he said over his shoulder. He looked for a good thinking stone – not that he had any doubts about it being time to go home, but what would he say to Voice?

He tried several stones, but none of them really helped.

"Perhaps you're not ready."

Jimmy jumped.

"Oh, sorry: Bing-Bong. Sorry mate. You were miles away, weren't you? But that's the Wilderness for you – you're missing your Molly, aren't you."

"Are you at it again?"

"Well, that's not difficult, is it? That hardly takes divine inspiration, does it?"

"Is she missing me?"

"No, I told you, it doesn't work that way. But it is nearly time to go."

"What – the wedding?"

"Yeah, nearly."

"I was supposed to book the cars."

"Don't worry. Stop panicking."

"When is the wedding?"

"Tomorrow. One more night, and tomorrow morning."

There was silence for a long time. Eventually Voice said, "You're not ready, are you?"

"Ready for what?"

"Exactly… You've got a lot of work to do, haven't you."

"I wish everybody would stop saying that!"

"Yeah, I know… Look, I haven't got time now. I've got to go. There's a bit of a do tonight. Well, it's a big do, actually. I've been planning this for some time."

"You're having a party? Any chance of an invite? I could do with a bit of a…"

"No. No you can't. And it's not my party. But it's a big do, and all the fairies are going, and I'll tell you Jim, some of them are bang…" Voice stopped himself.

"What?"

"Oh yeah, you better believe it. And there's one going – the spitting image of Madonna… and that's your Madonna, not our one," he quickly added. "And I've been working on this for the last two hundred and fifty years. And tonight's the night."

"You sly dog, Voicie!"

"Oh, you're dead right there. I've used every trick in the book and a few more of my own. You want to see her, Jimmy – but of course you can't. But if you could… she's gorgeous.

Won hairstyle of the month three times."

"Well you'd better go and get ready then."

"Yeah, you're right. See you in the morning." Voicie left, leaving Jimmy wondering how somebody who's invisible actually gets ready.

* * *

That evening, there was a bit more bounce in his step, despite the unknown burden he was apparently carrying. He prepared his chicken in barbecue sauce *à la Souvlaki*. Jimmy may well have prepared a chicken *à la Souvlaki* before, which perhaps slipped his mind, and he was more than entitled to some sympathy in this respect, considering that tiny part of Jimmy's anatomy which we may refer to as his mind was somewhat overcrowded.

I wouldn't mind a permanent job here, he thought. *I wonder how you become an archangel? Two hundred and fifty years, eh – and tonight's the night. Better find out what this work is I'm supposed to be doing and get it boxed off quick.*

He planned an early night so he could attack the next day with renewed vigour, but then Bear arrived, also in need of an early night. But instead of their early night they chatted into the early hours, both excited about their future prospects.

"I'm pretty good at pecking prosses," said Prima Donna, who had just wandered in thinking there was a party, "if you tell me what a prosses is."

Jimmy was still fast asleep in the morning when Voice arrived.

"Come on, Jimmy! Get up!"

Jimmy got up quickly, dying to hear all the gory details, leaving Bear still fast asleep in the cave.

"OK, Voice. How did the party go? Don't miss out a single detail."

"Didn't go."

"What! Why?"

"Well, you need more time."

"Time? But we haven't got any more time, have we – the wedding's today!"

"I've put it off."

"What!"

"Well, not put it off, exactly. I've frozen it. And believe me, that's a biggie – it took some doing, I can tell you."

Jimmy was stunned into silence.

"To stop time for a few moments, that's OK, that's routine – we all do it – but to stop it for a couple of days is big stuff. I had to pull on every favour I had owing, and then some. As you can imagine, all the angels have their customers and their schedules."

Jimmy tried to imagine but got absolutely nowhere.

"So I had to let my ticket to the party go, to buy credits."

"What, for me?"

"Well, it's not just for you. It's me as well."

Jimmy felt quite moved, quite emotional. Such a sacrifice. "Thanks Bear," said Jimmy, totally confused about everything – not least about who he was talking to.

Voice let it slip. He understood how the whole thing could be a bit mind-blowing.

"Well, it is very kind of you," said Jimmy, thinking he should sound grateful, "but, erm…"

"No buts, but perhaps I should mention, though… it wasn't entirely my idea; you've made quite an impact up here – well, up there… same thing."

"Yeah, well that'll be the, er… Why?"

"Oh yes, impact's the word. Everybody's talking with a Scouse accent these days, and Scouse jokes are quite the thing. I told them that joke of yours about the gay and the ball of wool."

"What joke about the gay and the ball of wool?"

"You know, someone wrote on the toilet wall."

Jimmy looked confused.

"You know – when we were talking about Billy – someone wrote on the toilet wall MY MOTHER MADE ME GAY, and someone wrote underneath IF I SEND HER THE WOOL WILL SHE MAKE ME ONE? Went straight to Number One."

"I never told you that!"

"Didn't you? Wow! Must be me. I must be becoming a Scouser. Wow! So, anyway, I've been asked to work with you for the next two or three days, so when we get back we can hit the ground running, as it were."

"So you are coming back with me, then?"

"Well, no. Not exactly. It's more the royal we, which means you go back and you do the running bit."

"Running? Running where? I've never been that good at running."

"Don't underestimate yourself. You can run. Everybody can run. And that's what we've got to do over the next couple of days – make sure we're running in the right direction… royal we."

Though Voice had said a couple of days, it wasn't actually two days as is generally understood; time didn't exist as is generally understood. They had stuff to do, and when it was done it was done.

And so the work began.

* * *

They walked around and about for a while so Jimmy could have another go at finding a good thinking stone to sit on. Eventually they found one – not a particularly good thinking stone, but Voice was getting impatient and Jimmy was getting a bit knackered, so it had to do.

"So. The Big Guy," said Voice, "He put in place in the

beginning, in the very beginning, a need, a desire, within each and every person to leave the world a better place – a law of the universe, if you like. And so it was set as one of the fundamental needs of man. But…" Voice noticed a lightbulb appear above Jimmy's head, "Yes, Jimmy?"

"Well," said Jimmy with a pretty well-if-that's-the-case-why-is-the-world-in-such-shit-order look on his face.

"Exactly," said Voice. "Exactly," he repeated. "Why indeed?"

Jimmy's face changed to well-that's-what-I-said-and-seeing-I-asked-first…

"OK, OK. Well, who do you know who's going to leave the world a better place?"

Jimmy thought for quite some time. "I know. That builder guy – what's his name? Cooper. That's him, George Cooper. He's done alright for himself – big house, made lots of money, and he built the new leisure centre."

"OK, the leisure centre. Have a word with Daisy when you get back. And doing alright for himself – is that it? Is that going to qualify for leaving the world a better place? It would be easier," said Voice, thinking it would be worth throwing in a biblical reference at this point, "It would be easier for a camel to piss through the eye of a needle than for a rich man to enter the Kingdom of Heaven."

"That's not right!"

"Oh, yes it is! That's my department, don't forget. That's why we don't get many rich men in heaven. Don't get many camels, either – though I'm not sure it's related."

"It's pass."

"Don't be soft! That doesn't make sense: it would be easier for the camel to piss through the pass. Anyone can do that," Voicie chuckled.

So did Jimmy, "I agree – but that's not the saying. It's 'it would be easier for a camel to PASS through the eye of a needle than for a rich man', blah blah."

There was a silence as Voicie's invisible mouse ran round his invisible wheel. "Well, doggone! I think you're right! Where did you learn that?"

"I don't know. Back of the cornflakes, I suppose."

"Cornflakes, hey? Must get some of them."

"Don't you have cornflakes?"

"Oh, yes, they're there – they've gone all modern these days – you know, buffet help yourself thing. I've been having fruit and yoghurt lately, you know – piling on the pounds a bit as the years roll by. … So, doing alright for yourself isn't going to get you the ticket, is it."

It carried on on this tack for some time.

"Oh, I can't do this!" said Jimmy.

"Oh, yes you can!"

"No, you've got the wrong man. My job is to make boxes… and shout myself dry at Anfield… and get pissed in the Duck House. That's me."

"No, Jimmy. Too late – you've already started. You remember that old couple in the park?"

"What old couple in the park?"

"You know, when you were talking with Billy, telling Billy he was giving it one… funny, that!"

"Oh, that was a mistake! They weren't supposed to be overhearing that."

"Well, she's pregnant."

"What!"

"Yeah, baby in the Spring."

"What!!"

"And she wants you to be godfather."

"What!!!"

"God, Jimmy! She's eighty-four! You are in a bad way, aren't you."

Now, for the sake of any puritanicals who might be reading

this and think Voice has just been guilty of blasphemy, it was decided in H some time ago that in certain circumstances, and if a point needed enforcing, it was OK to use the G word, and of course following the maxim that there's no such thing as bad publicity.

Voice, seeing the need to pull Jimmy back from the brink, as it were, said, "What really swung it your way was the Osama Bin Laden thing."

Jimmy looked drained. *Where's he going now?*

"That took some bottle, that did. Albeit you got the wrong Greek island, and nearly killed a priest, but some bottle."

"Well," said Jimmy, "I've got to own up to it, I was looking for the glory."

"OK, we won't include that one then."

"Well, hang on a minute, there was a certain amount of… No," he corrected himself, "there was actually a good deal of ridding the world of an evil tyrant. That had to be good for mankind, didn't it? And I helped George Cooper get his cat out of the tree…" He related several more instances to illustrate that if the world was in shit order it wasn't down to him. Oh no. Trying to convince himself, as much as Voice, that he'd done his bit.

The day went on in much the same vein.

Jimmy got back to his cave drained and exhausted, and slept and slept. He dreamed there were fairies at the bottom of his garden. The dream was so real, as dreams often are, but this was really real. Even when he woke and got up he could still see them, and even when they gradually disappeared into the reality of the Wilderness he could close his eyes and back they would come.

When Voice arrived, Jimmy told him about his dream. Voice was very impressed.

"We must be getting very close, Jimmy."

"Close?"

"Yes, I agree."

"I mean close to what, plonker? And fairies at the bottom of the garden? I mean, that was a dream. I mean… fairies don't exist do they?"

Voice looked a bit hurt, but he managed to hide it – which wasn't too difficult, being invisible and all.

"Of course they do. You saw them."

"Yes, but that was just a dream."

"But your dream was very real. What's the difference between that reality and the reality you're seeing now? If it all seemed very real, how d'you know it wasn't real? I mean, at the time you believed it to be real and, if you accept that, what else is there? The only world that isn't real is what people refer to as the 'real world' – that's the false one."

"You've got a point there, Voice," Jimmy looked around at the Wilderness, wondering if there was anywhere he could get some paracetamol. "Have you seen them? Of course you have. I meant have you got them at the bottom of your garden?"

Now Voice had a far away look in his eyes with a touch of sadness. "Used to, Jimmy. Used to. Not for a long time now. Not since that unfortunate incident behind the potting shed… which, incidentally, was blown up out of all proportion. But that was a long time ago. They'll be back. But… but… but back to business. Now who can tell me what we've learned so far?"

He was met with silence.

"… I'm talking to you, Jimmy."

Jimmy knew that, but had hoped somebody else would chip in because when he looked into his memory all he could see was tumbleweed drifting across a desert.

Voice decided to change tack. "What if," he said, "we were to give the old man in Corfu a very large sum of money. What would he do? Would he buy a new donkey – a younger one? One he could ride, or perhaps pull a cart – with his old donkey in the back of the cart with his little dog? Or perhaps he could buy a motorized truck, and learn to drive, and he won't need a donkey at all."

"Oh, he needs his donkey."

"Yes, of course he does. Well, perhaps if his pot of money was big enough he could pay someone else to look after his salad garden."

"No way," said Jimmy.

"No?" said Voice.

"Not going to work, is it!" they both said together.

"So he doesn't want anything?" said Jimmy after some time.

"Oh yes, though want is perhaps the wrong word; need might be a better one. He needs a purpose, a function, a reason for being."

"He's got his veg patch – and his donkey and his dog need him."

"Not enough. Remember when he gave you the salad?"

"Yes, of course I do."

"And you were very grateful, weren't you."

"Yes, of course I was. It was good of him. He was a good old stick."

"Yes, well I know you know all that. And you know it meant a lot to him as well. He could have given it to anybody, couldn't he – or not bothered at all. But he chose you. And when you were hurrying back to the beach he knew you were running late. It doesn't matter whether that short cut existed or not. He wanted to help. And he knew you knew he wanted to help. And he also knew you were grateful, and that gave him purpose, a reason for being. He probably got more out of it than you did."

Jimmy reflected. The kindness of strangers. And I still need paracetamol.

"What's that old wives' saying, better to give than to receive. Can't wait to get old Daisy up in H. I bet she's got some crackers. Though I will wait," added Voice quickly, "No rush."

And so they walked and talked, and talked and walked.

"So, doing alright for yourself is a load of crap?"

"If you like, but it's up to you to work it out for yourself."

"Oh, come on – you're supposed to be helping me out here!"

"Alright then. What's the point of having the big house if you have a gardener looking after your veg patch? And all you're worried about is whether you might lose your empire one day… Who get's the biggest buzz – Richard Branson sending a 747 across the Atlantic, or the old man watching his row of seedlings coming up in the spring?

"And the old man gave you the salad. You wouldn't be given a free ticket on the plane, would you, unless you gave something back in return, in a material sense that is."

"I've had money in the past – I've wasted a lot of my money."

"Yes, a fool and his money are soon parted; but it's a bigger fool who's frightened of letting go of it."

Jimmy stared at Voice – or at least would have done if he knew where he was. "That was nearly very good!"

"It was, wasn't it!"

Jimmy wasn't quite sure what it meant, but the phrase wouldn't leave him alone. All his life he'd believed that money was the solution to everything, but then as soon as he had some there was something else needed – always something else.

"Now you're getting it, Jimmy lad."

"What am I getting?"

"Exactly. So, if it's not the solution, it's got to be part of the problem."

Jimmy wished he'd found the paracetamol.

"Well, it's got to be one or the other, hasn't it?"

"You mean it's not *not* having any money – it's the *fear* of not having any money. Is that the problem?"

"Exactly. Couldn't have put it better myself."

What have I just said? He racked his brains to remember, but it wasn't happening.

"Fear, Jimmy."

"Fear. Is that it? Is that all it is?"

"Oh, don't underestimate fear – it's very powerful – but money isn't the solution to the fear, it's a contributor. People believe that owning the big house, the big car, is success – it's not. The big house owns them, with the maintenance, insurance, gardeners, cleaners, burglar alarms, all adding to the fear. Anything you buy comes with a cost, a responsibility, a duty of care. Paying for it does not give you ownership – that's just the down payment. The only thing you truly own is yourself."

Jimmy found an interesting pebble on the ground, and wandered around looking for another one.

"What's your greatest fear?"

"Fear? Are we still on about that?"

"Yes, of course we are. What's your greatest fear?"

"Liverpool losing in the European Cup final."

"Come on, Jimmy, concentrate."

They walked on in silence for a while.

"I'd say snuffing it before the kids could cope, I suppose, though Sinead's getting married… and Molly, losing Molly."

"Ah, fear and love. The two most powerful emotions. Nothing to do with money, though. Money can't buy you love."

"But what about all the poverty, all the poor people? They need money."

"Ah, yes! But the same thing applies. Money is a curved ball. What's needed is balance, harmony in the world. Truth, honesty, kindness – all that sort of stuff. That's where you come in. I would suggest you start with greed – the lust for money – the rest will follow."

"What! Me come in? How? Why? Me? Who?"

"Slow down! Slow down, Jimmy. But you're right – it's a biggie. Money's a powerful drug. That's why it's there. But it's a curved ball. It's a test, it's there to see how many people fall into the trap, and how many have the guts to find that out and do something about it."

Jimmy looked dazed.

"But there are the perks, though."

"What!!"

"Don't get excited… or perhaps you should – it's brilliant. First of all, you get a decent job when you get up to H…"

"What?"

"…Yes, of course. Everything you do on earth adds to your c.v., as it were, and gives you the pecking order on the next bit."

"What, like an archangel?"

"Ah, well don't get carried away. That's pretty high up."

"You did it."

"Yeah, well I was a decent bloke. Gave a few of the bad guys a bloody nose, that sort of stuff – but they don't like me saying that."

"Oh, I see. They don't like you bragging?"

"No. They don't like the word bloke. It's a bit, well, bloke-ish. But the real trick is to get the rewards while you're still here – on earth, that is – but that's for you to find out."

"But what d'you mean, rewards… What are the perks?"

"Oh, there's loads. I can work it so you've got free socks for life."

"What?"

"Well you know all the socks that go missing in the washing machine or something? Well… we've got them. Millions of them. It started off as a bit of a joke, but what it does, it just keeps people guessing. They search and search for the socks and they never find them. So they constantly wonder where they've gone. So, anyway, I'll see to it you get all the socks. All the socks you'll ever need.

"…And pencils… and pens," he added, as an afterthought. "We've got an enormous wardrobe up in H, full of partly used pens and pencils. Might come in handy, seeing you're writing a book."

The thought of free socks for life occupied Jimmy's mind for quite some time, it just wouldn't go away. He knew socks went missing, of course, but hadn't really given it a lot of thought, because any shortage there might have been was dealt with every Christmas.

"But we're going off the subject. Greed. Corruption."

"But how am I going to stop all the greed?"

"Don't know – we've been trying for two thousand years – that's not the point. But millions could. That's why the Big Guy kicked off. The vast majority of people are decent folk. The evil ones – the corrupt businessmen, politicians – carry on as if it's all OK, with the inevitable consequences – bullying, dishonesty… All the millions know it's going on but pretend they don't, scared of the consequences, but what they refuse to acknowledge is there aren't any, if they just had the guts. And so they go through their day with their head buried in the sand. But that's just as bad, and subconsciously they know that."

"And how am I supposed to change all that on my own?"

"Exactly…"

For a nano-moment, Jimmy thought he'd been let off the hook.

"…but that's just a cop-out…

"The interesting thing, though – it gets them nowhere. All the so-called clever blokes are just running round like headless chickens… sorry, Prima Donna… like lemmings searching for the edge. And that's another interesting thing – lemmings got the idea of leaping off the edge from those blokes, but, being more intelligent than those blokes, they bypassed the big houses and fast cars – and just went straight for the edge.

"…And another interesting thing is, you're not on your own. Everybody has their own archangel – their own oracle – and you can talk to the oracle whenever you want to and wherever you are. The oracle doesn't lie, doesn't boast, doesn't have an ego to satisfy, no ulterior motive: it just is. Everybody's private source of wisdom."

"A coracle's a little round boat – what the hell's that got to do with it?"

"It's not a coracle, goon! It's an oracle! Concentrate, Jimmy – this is important, this bit."

"I know, I know! Keep your hair on! Just having a joke."

Jimmy's thoughts drifted, *has Voicie got hair? What's his hair like? Never really thought of that before.*

"Interesting point, that, Jimmy. You might have something here."

"What, about your hair?"

"No! The coracle. That's exactly what it's like! The oracle inside is like a little round boat. When you find the oracle, jump in and let the coracle take you where it wants to go. Very clever that. Well done, Jimmy."

"Yeah, well…"

"Don't gloat… That's what you've got to do, though: find the oracle and get yourself on the road to Damascus, and that's about it. And by the way I have quite nice hair."

Jimmy, eager to come up with something intelligent again to keep his ego fed, said, "Er… Damascus? That's near Corfu, isn't it?"

"No, it's in Syria, but this isn't a geography lesson. You'll know when you're on it – you'll see this light thing – I think that's how it happens. Anyway, you'll know. And when you find the oracle you'll be able to tell others where it is.

"My old mother used to say the more Indians you can bring to the teepee the less chance of the peace pipe going out. Funny woman."

"You have a mother?"

Chapter 21

When Jimmy got back to his cave he wasn't tired. No exhaustion like the day before. For some reason, he felt renewed, despite the several hedges he had been dragged through. A lot of what Voice had said seemed to make sense. Perhaps he did have a purpose in the scheme of things. But he slept anyway, a deep, peaceful sleep, until Voice came bouncing in:

"Who's the angel? Voicie's the angel!
Who's the angel? Voicie's the angel!"

"What are you so bouncy about?"

"It's my saying: 'a fool and his money are soon parted, but it's a bigger fool who's frightened of letting go of it'. It's gone straight to number one. Never had a number one before – never had one in the top five before!"

Jimmy and Voicie danced around, singing, "Who's the angel? Voicie's the angel!" which woke Bear up, who came and joined in though he wasn't quite sure why, then went back to bed.

Jimmy decided to throw a party – a farewell party – seeing this was his last night. He invited Prima Donna, and said to Bear, with some trepidation, "Why not bring Sassy?"

"Oh, can I?" said Bear. "She's such a beautiful bear, and you know when she hugs you…" Bear stopped himself, which did nothing to ease Jimmy's apprehension. Still, the invitation was there.

He asked Prima Donna to come round an hour early with the hope that she would arrive about the same time as Bear.

As sod's law works in the Wilderness, the same as everywhere else, Prima Donna arrived at her allotted time, which meant that she and Jimmy could have a quiet chat before Bear and Sassy arrived.

"I'm going to miss you, Jimmy."

"I'm going to miss you too, my little feathered friend... well, nearly feathered." Jimmy was feeling a bit, well... at Prima Donna's remark.

"I've never told anybody the true story about Antony before. Do you think I will meet him again? I mean, you know, in Free Range – I mean heaven – there is a heaven, isn't there?"

"Yeah, I'm sure there is." He thought for a long time, and then repeated, "Yeah, I'm sure there is. Never used to. Never really gave it a lot of thought before, but I've learned a lot since I've been in the Wilderness... a hell of a lot. Do you wish you'd gone with him?"

"Sometimes, yes, but I was frightened."

I think I should point out that the Free Range Prima Donna is referring to is not the free range referred to on Earth. The definition of free range on Earth is considered something of a joke in heaven; battery hens are produced for no other reason than cooking, whereas free range gives the chicken a reason for living – a reason for being – and then cook it. The dictionary in heaven lists this as an example of stupidity. It's also listed to illustrate the definition of self-delusion, along with the human race considering itself intelligent.

Jimmy was starting to understand what Prima Donna was feeling. He'd taken Molly for granted for years, and now he missed her so much it was like an ache that wouldn't go away. Things were going to be so different when he got back home. A tear came into his eye. He put his arm around Prima Donna and they both sat there quietly, each drifting within their own thoughts.

"D'you believe in fairies?" said Prima Donna, "You know, they live at the bottom of your garden? Only, last night I had a weird dream. I was playing with the fairies at the bottom of the garden, and you were there too. It was so real: when I woke up I could still see them."

They sat there quietly, each wandering into memories of their past, their present, and their plans for the future. Suddenly, Jimmy felt Prima Donna tense. She stood up and stared along the path between the rocks that led to the Wilderness next door.

"What's the matter?"

But she wasn't listening. Her face, her eyes fierce, focused on the gap in the rocks, every sinew, every muscle in her body taught like a drum. Her beak stretched out like an arrow waiting to fly, her right claw scratching the ground. Then Bear appeared around the rock with Sassy. Sassy was wearing a feather boa made out of chicken feathers.

With an ear-piercing screech, Prima Donna flew at her.

"No! No! No!" shouted Jimmy.

Chapter 22

"It's no good saying no now," said Molly, "We decided, and that's that. Jack Butler's going with you. Anyway, Terry's gone round to get him now."

There was a knock on the door.

"Look, that'll be Billy and Dimitri. You go and have a good time. I'm not going to bother saying don't get drunk. I'll be wasting me time. Just remember we've got a wedding in the morning."

I'm not bothered, thought Jimmy, *that Jack Butler's going to be there*. But he was, just a bit. He opened the door.

"Dimitri! Good to see you! You've come for our big fat Liverpool wedding, have you?"

He hadn't seen Jack Butler for months, hadn't discussed any of the arrangements. Let sleeping dogs lie, he'd said to Molly, but *is he going to be pissed off that I've taken it on myself to do up the loft for Sinead and Terry without consulting him?* Jack could be a bit of a handful. Was there an animal lying dormant in there? If it was going to growl, it would probably be tonight.

They went to the Duck House first. *Best on home turf*, he thought.

It started off OK. "Good to see you, Jimmy lad," said Jack Butler.

There were twelve lads altogether, mostly Terry's mates. Three pints then down to the Greyhound.

Jimmy went straight to the toilet in the Greyhound, followed by Jack. You could say it was something of a captive audience: two men standing alongside each other, relieving themselves.

"I was hoping to have a quiet word with you, Jimmy."

It was nothing to do with Jimmy's being nervous that made him splash his polished shoes a bit. That was just coincidence.

"...About our Terry and your lass. It's good of you, pal – you and Molly. I believe you've done a bit of a room up in your loft."

"No, it wasn't me, they did it themselves. Decent joiner, your Terry, isn't he."

They'd been in the toilet for four, nearly five, minutes, and Billy had been staring at the door for the last couple. *If he's going to give Jimmy a kicking*, he thought, *he's going to have to give me one as well*, and burst in.

"Ah, Billy lad!" said Jack. "We were just having a discussion over who's round it is, and it turns out to be mine, doesn't it Jimmy."

"Yeah, that's right," Jimmy nodded, with some relief.

Jack and Jimmy sat together after that, and an unlikely friendship blossomed.

"He's alright, Billy, isn't he?" said Jack.

"Ah, he'll do."

"No, took some bottle that, bringing Dimitri here. Not sure I could do it if I was a poofter. No, he's alright, Billy."

Jimmy was a bit open-mouthed at the frankness. Prior to that night they hadn't said two words to each other.

"There was a poofter used to go down to the gym, you know when I was doing a bit of the boxing. God, he was a hard lad. Used to hate fighting him. Couldn't put him down... kept coming back. Couldn't put him down, Jimmy."

"You put a few down, though, didn't you. Regional champion, weren't you?"

"Behave yourself! I was going to be British champion. Said

197

so on the back of my shirt. Everybody kept telling me. And I knew I could have been, anyway. Trouble was, I took it for granted, expected it to come easy. Started drinking the medicine." He downed his pint, "Long time ago."

Jimmy found himself fighting a compulsion to start talking about the meaning of life and the whole point of it all, with little success. "So your ex isn't coming tomorrow?"

"Annette? No, not coming. Thank God! Still a bit raw, though it's been six years now. Should never have got married."

Terry was made up to see his dad getting on so well with Jimmy.

"He's alright, your old feller," Jimmy said to Terry when he caught up with him at the bar.

Jack and Jimmy were allowed to carry on their private conversation. After all, they were the two oldies.

"Still, our two seem to have got it right, don't you think?" said Jack.

"Yeah, looks like, as far as you can tell."

"You and Molly must have got married pretty young?"

"Yeah, but it's not always cast in stone, is it. You and Annette never worked out?"

"No, never should have got married. I was winning a few fights, the girls were around. Thought I was God's Gift, started drinking. Anyway, she pissed off with some twat from Birkenhead six years ago. Anyway, they went to live in Spain, left me with Terry."

"Pretty tough… so, she's not coming tomorrow."

"No, she's probably frightened I'll give him a smack."

"You wouldn't, would you?"

"No. Might give him a tap, though. He's a cunt, Jimmy. He thinks because he's got a couple of properties on the Costa del Plonka he's the big tycoon. Anyway, as you know, the kids are going out there for a few days after the wedding. They've got a place for them, apparently – their wedding present."

* * *

So Dimitri led the Greek dancing, smashed a few plates, Terry got pissed, and Jimmy found a new mate. A good night.

* * *

Much to Molly's surprise, Jimmy was up bright and early the next morning – in the back yard, scribbling on bits of paper, working on his speech. The service went off without a hitch, everybody raving about the dresses – even Molly's sister Celia thought they looked quite nice, though she had to throw in Her Jeremy and his fiancee were going to a bridal shop in Altrincham. Daisy had to get a hankie out of her pocket three times during the service, though she would deny it. JJ collected the confetti off the ground to throw it again for the third time, which amounted to half confetti, half gravel and half muck.

As Jimmy got into the full flow of his speech, Sinead whispered to her mother, "What's me dad going on about with these Indians and teepees?"

"I haven't the faintest idea, love, and I'm not going to ask him. It's obviously some sort of mid-life crisis."

There was polite applause, but nobody really got the point of all Jimmy's hard work.

"Don't let him start drinking Stella, Mam."

"Don't worry. Billy and Dimitri have got their instructions."

What Molly hadn't reckoned with, though, was Jack Butler – Jimmy's new best friend – who could match Jimmy pint for pint any day of the week. But Jimmy stayed true to his promise and stayed away from the Stella. After all, it was his daughter's wedding. But, although the lager Jimmy settled for wasn't blessed with the same degree of potency as Stella, the same result could be reached by volume.

"That wasn't a bad speech, that," said Jack, "and I liked your poem."

Jimmy glowed, which got his adrenaline flowing along with the lager.

"I used to think it was just the boxing world that was corrupt," said Jack, "but it's the whole fucking world, isn't it."

Over in the corner were two of Sinead's teachers, Mr Hargreaves and Mr Evans, with their wives, sipping halves of lager, and chardonnay. Jimmy decided to go and test some of his theories on the intelligent sector of the gathering.

"I wonder if you could enlighten me," said Jimmy, putting on his most intelligent voice. "Me and my acquaintance over there were just discussing world affairs, and the way all the politicians and most of the businessmen are bent. I don't mean gay, like Dimitri and Billy – I mean corrupt – you know, bent. And we're not just talking about Sefton Park here. I mean the Middle East, Washington and Milton Keynes."

"Well, I don't think this is really the time or place…"

"Well, that's the trouble. People don't think. Don't you think that's the trouble – people don't think, or pretend not to think? Would you say you are an-in-head-sand-buried person from an educational point of view?"

"You mean does the education system have its head in the sand?"

"That's what I said."

"No, I wouldn't say that at all."

"Ah! Well, if you were an in-head-sand-buried person, you wouldn't admit it, would you."

The teachers were stunned into silence.

"Ah! I've got you there, haven't I!"

Jimmy, having now claimed the intellectual higher ground, decided to pursue another subject.

"What's your opinions on God? You know, the Big Guy, heaven, that sort of stuff."

Jimmy was met with blank disbelief.

"Well, to tell you the truth, what I was wondering is: where do you stand on trifles?" Jimmy roared with laughter. "Did you hear what I just said there: where do you stand on trifles!"

Mr Hargreaves had to laugh, and so did Mr Evans' wife, not that they knew what Jimmy was on about, but the way he went about it.

The conversation was interrupted as a very angry Molly burst in. "I'll give her bloody trifle!"

"What's happened?" said Jimmy.

"It's her. Bloody Celia, and her Jeremy's girlfriend – sorry, fiaaancay."

"What the hell's happened? What's going on?"

"I'll tell you what's going on! She's insinuating our Sinead had to get married, and the wedding was all rushed, and how their Jeremy's behaving much more responsibly. Saving up for a house, and THEN they'll get married. And THEN in a few years' time they'll start a family."

"She didn't say all that."

"Oh, yes she did – the bloody cow! Not in so many words, but with her sarcastic…"

"Oh dear," said Jimmy.

"I'll give her bloody trifle!" Molly stormed off to the buffet table, filled big bowl with fruit salad and cream, and headed back to find Celia, who in the meantime had gone for a walk in the garden.

Suddenly Celia came running back in, screaming hysterically. "There's a bear outside!" she screamed, "A big grizzly bear!" Her husband, Jeremy and fiancée tried to calm her down, but she wasn't having any. "There's a bear, an enormous bear! Call the police!"

Jimmy sobered up immediately and dashed over. "Where was it?"

"It was there!" she screamed through her hysteria, "There, sitting on the lawn," pointing through the window. "A giant bear!"

Everybody dashed over to look through the window. There was nothing there.

"You've imagined it, you soft cow!" said Molly, "Here, have some trifle."

She never intended to throw the whole bowl at Celia, just to fire a spoonful periodically at appropriate moments until the skirmish reached its artistic conclusion.

Jimmy managed to grab the bowl of fruit salad out of her hand and passed it to Jack Butler who was now standing alongside him.

"I'm not imagining it! It was sitting on the grass like a giant teddy bear, with a chicken…"

"With a chicken?" shouted Jimmy, his mind flying back to the Wilderness.

"Yes, with a chicken. I saw it clearly. The chicken had a feather boa."

"It's not a Grizzly Bear – it's a Brown Bear," spluttered Jimmy as he dashed outside, followed by Billy, Dimitri and Terry at some distance behind. But Bear and Prima Donna had gone.

Jack Butler sat down and ate the bowl of fruit salad. *Now it's a proper wedding*, he thought.

PART 3

THE ORACLE

Chapter 23

It would be impossible to say whether it was after the holiday or after Jimmy's time in the Wilderness, or the wedding maybe,
   that everything changed
   but remained the same
   though in a kind of a way it was different
   Did somebody say: *everything influences everything?*
   Molly rediscovering herself.

JJ growing into a young man, albeit for a short time, but perhaps showing us a glimpse of the man he would become.

Sinead able to start her new life in the total confidence that she had made the right decision.

Daisy moving her rocking chair from the verandah in the Mississippi to the living room where it was most needed, taking her rightful place in the scheme of things.

Billy released from the burden that an ignorant society had placed on him.

And Jimmy…

* * *

Sinead and Terry settled in to their loft apartment, Terry working hard doing foreigners whenever he could – weekends and sometimes of an evening. They wanted their own place. Sinead went back to college, though in a few months' time the baby would be due.

Molly put her designs and patterns back in the box, but they never found their way back to the loft – well, the loft wasn't there any more. She put them in a corner of the living room, but they didn't stay there for long, either.

"I'm going to make myself some new clothes, Mam."

"Good."

Fired by this note of approval, Molly and Daisy got the bus into town and went to the fabric shops. Molly had an idea of what she was looking for, but that all changed as soon as she started wandering around. As if driven by some unforeseen force, within a few minutes she knew exactly what she was looking for.

"How about this one?" said Daisy, "Make a nice blouse."

"No, not quite."

"Well, what about this one, then? She pulled the bolt of cloth off the rail, "You could probably get two, or three…"

"Erm… erm… no, no… Let's go and have a cup of coffee and I'll tell you what I'm after."

Molly scribbled a sketch on a napkin – a gypsy-style top that could be off the shoulder or not – and waited for the disapproval, which didn't happen. The years had been kind to Molly; despite two children she'd kept her figure, unlike most of the mothers. She carried on with a few more scribbles.

After they'd finished their toasted teacake and cup of tea, Daisy said, "Well, you'd better put them back in your bag. People steal stuff like that, you know."

Jimmy still went to work at Maddens, but not by car. He still had his car but chose to go by bus. Billy went with him, but for how long? He had started going to evening classes to learn Greek.

Jimmy's memory of his time in the Wilderness was fast disappearing, like a dream that was so vivid in the morning but, no matter how hard you try to keep hold of it, it runs through your fingers like sand, just leaving a few fragments of the story.

He decided, before anyone knew, that his grandchild was going to be a girl, and started carving a little girl out of wood. She would sit on a swing and act as one half of the balance to the scales he was working on, the other half being a house plant. *Hibiscus,* he thought, *though it may not survive round here.* Anyway, the plant would rise and fall, indicating the need for watering.

Carving a girl that was to sit on a swing was just about the most difficult task Jimmy had ever undertaken; he'd never tried anything so complicated before, and getting the proportions right took a massive amount of concentration. To add to his persecution, he chose to carve her out of an old piece of spalted beech, full of worm holes and rotten bits. At one point her left arm fell off, but he carried on, keeping her arm to repair later. Then her head fell off while he was shaping the legs. Undaunted, he carried on.

"Why don't you start again with a new bit?" said Molly.

"No, it was my fault. I made her neck too thin. I can repair that as well."

"Tell me about it!" Molly muttered.

Molly knew exactly what Jimmy was going through. She had never bought sewing patterns if she could possibly avoid it; she adapted ones that were there from years ago, or just made her own. She really had little choice, because all her designs were original. She showed Jimmy a top she'd just made.

"Hey, that's alright, isn't it!"

"You don't think it's a bit, well…"

"No! Go for it girl."

She was wearing her new top and long skirt when Sinead came home.

"Oh, I like that. BoHo."

"What?"

"You know! Bohemian Romantic?"

Molly didn't know; she'd never heard that expression before. *Mm, I rather like that though*, she thought, *yeah… Bohemian Romantic.*

The hours and weeks Jimmy had already spent on his carving didn't matter. Perhaps many more hours and weeks to go. At some stage his girl on the swing had to balance with the plant, and how heavy was the plant? He didn't even know how heavy his sculpture was going to be. He did know what the plant container looked like; it was leather, or leatherette probably, with a pull cord round the top, and that had to be made. Time ceased to have the same meaning as it had a few months ago. It was as though he'd crossed over to a different dimension.

The back yard became Jimmy's sanctuary, his place of peace. The total absorption in his sculpture left his mind to wander wherever it decided to go without him having to drive it. Also, a blessed escape from the living room that from time to time became a sewing factory.

JJ saw any changes in the dynamic of the household as of little consequence, knowing that if there were any perceived changes in the hierarchy of the pecking order it was temporary, and continued to throw all his allegiance on the side of his father, knowing normal service would be resumed sooner or later, apart from his sister, who was more or less taken out of the equation for the foreseeable future, albeit by just one flight of stairs. That had to be an improvement in any assessment.

Nevertheless, Daisy, to make sure no permanent psychological damage could occur to him by being left out of all the changes, suggested to JJ that his dad could make him a boat, a wooden boat to sail on the lake. Daisy was quite good at drawing, and with the help of JJ, she sketched a boat. It would be about twelve inches long with two funnels. When Jimmy saw the sketch, "What a good idea," he said, "Yes, I can make that," thinking a boat was much easier to make than his current project and a welcome excuse to leave that one alone for a while. The fishing boat, for that was what Jimmy was now calling it, looked great, and JJ loved it. Though Daisy pointed out several times that it was more like ten inches long and not twelve, and only had one funnel not two, which raised some argument on three occasions; Daisy saying that Jimmy didn't fulfil the design brief, and Jimmy pointing out that in contract law the agreement between father and son is reasonably flexible vis-à-vis the length department, and also vis-à-vis the number of funnels department, and, as the contract was between father and son, kindly butt out.

So came the day of the launch. It was still to be painted, but it could be checked to make sure it was seaworthy. Jimmy was reasonably confident on that point, having bobbed it about in the sink, so the whole family was there, by the lake, complete with picnic. The boat slowly moved off exactly as expected, gracefully rising and falling with the gentle ripples of the lake.

One thing that Jimmy didn't anticipate, though, was that well-made didn't necessarily mean well-behaved. The boat gradually drifted further and further out with nothing whatsoever to prevent it.

"It'll drift back in a minute," but Jimmy was convincing no-one, not even himself. The one minute turned into one hour, then three hours.

The sky went dark, and it began to rain. Everybody left the park and went home, including the family, apart from Jimmy and JJ. The rain turned into a storm as they watched their little boat being tossed around, battered by the rain.

"Look, Dad! It's trying to get to the island."

"It's got to be careful of those rocks, though, lad."

They were soaked through, but still they watched their boat fight its way through the rocks, then eventually run aground on the bank of the island roughly in the middle of the lake. They knew that, because they'd walked round the lake three times to see which was the shortest route back home, but they couldn't decide. Eventually, they were satisfied the boat was safe for the night, and they headed home.

On the way back the idea came to use JJ's fishing rod. Who had the idea first was a matter of some dispute. Nevertheless, that's what they decided to do.

Fishing was actually prohibited on the lake but, as they were not actually fishing for fish but fishing for a boat, they didn't think the ban applied to them. Nevertheless, to avoid any confrontation they went back at six o'clock the next morning. By eight-thirty JJ had successfully hooked the boat and they brought it safely back.

JJ and Daisy painted the boat, and it did look rather grand. Jimmy explained to JJ that sometimes life throws up something unexpected. The important thing is that you don't think of it as being devastating; everything has a solution. So now it was time for the true maiden voyage and, being a boat of such magnificence, she had to have a name. Several names were bandied about but, with a bit of careful manipulation, JJ decided to call the boat 'Sassy'.

And so, one week later, our family had another picnic by the lake. Now with fishing line tied to the front – sorry, bow – which allowed her to drift right out as far as her inclination took her and be brought back safely.

After several more trips to the lake with Sassy, she then took pride of place on JJ's windowsill. Jimmy mused, while working on his sculpture and thinking about the fishing rod and line having a function after all, *that's got to constitute a movement in a mysterious way, a mini one.*

* * *

All of his total absorption in the time Jimmy spent nibbling away at his wood was not governed by the usual motivations, like money or massaging his ego by receiving admiration from others, but it did give him time to think. *Recreation equals re-creation*, he thought, as the sculpture started to take shape. He often took his thoughts down to the lake to find bits of old wood and, if there was nobody about, he'd sit and talk to the ducks. They knew all about the fishing boat, and how the boat knew the storm was coming but it had to get to the island, it just had to.

He still went down to the Duck House with Billy, though he didn't drink as much these days. He still had a laugh and a joke with the lads, though he didn't find it necessary to be chief comedian all the time.

He asked one or two what they thought about love, marriage, and the point of it all. This started out as a bit of a joke, but then others came up to him saying, "Ask me the questions." He was moved at how seriously and honestly they responded, considering he was talking about love and marriage, and the point of it all – not the usual topic of conversation in the Duck House.

His main buddy for this philosophical diarrhoea was Jack Butler. "You should write the book," he'd said.

He had often thought of writing a book. He'd always made up stories for the kids, and occasionally they got written down, but a book?

* * *

"I'm thinking of writing a book."

"Good. About time." Molly went to the drawer, took out a notepad and a pencil, and handed them to Jimmy.

"I didn't mean right now." He put the notebook in his pocket.

On Saturday morning, instead of going down to the paper

shop, Jimmy went to the lake. He remembered Nikolas had told him to write the book, and the painting Nikolas had given him of an old Welsh fisherman.

He got to the lake deep in thought, totally oblivious of the ducks.

"Quack, Jimmy, quack-quack."

"Quack! Quack-quack. Morning!"

"Be like that then! Quack."

Jimmy walked on, unaware that he had snubbed his companions, and sat on a bench.

He'd decided to write his story through the eyes of the old fisherman, and began scribbling in his notebook. He'd been at it for some time before he realised he had an audience. A few ducks had forgiven him and gathered on the edge of the lake nearby, watching. When Jimmy had first arrived and ignored them, one or two had said, "Well, stuff him then, quack," and, "If he can't be bothered, then, quack." But then curiosity got the better of them.

Jimmy got up and went and sat at the edge of the bank and began to tell the ducks the story.

"It all started many many years ago in a small village in North Wales. Life was hard, and if the fishermen didn't catch any fish they went hungry. It was winter, and storms could happen any time. Still the boat went out. There were just five men on the boat, including skipper, Hywel Jones, the oldest and the most experienced."

One or two more ducks arrived to listen to the story, but the rest had more important things to do.

"The boat went on and on through the night, but in the distance they could hear the storm. Some of the men said 'we should turn back', but Hywel insisted and they went on, into the storm. The little boat was tossed about and was heading towards the rocks at the edge of an island way out at sea. It took all the strength of the five men to stop the boat being bashed and smashed to bits. The boat eventually ran aground on the banks of the island, and there they stayed until the early hours of the morning when the storm had passed. The tide lifted the boat and they began to make their way home, but without any fish. 'Let's try the nets one more time,' said Hywel. They were tired and exhausted, and they just wanted to get home, but the skipper insisted. The nets quickly became full of fish, and they caught as much as the little boat would carry. It was becoming light when they got back. The whole village was out on the pebble beach waiting for them. Some had been there for hours as they, too, had seen the storm. They screamed and cheered as the boat arrived, wives and girlfriends wiping away tears. Then everything went black, and silent, and still, frozen in time. Nobody moved except Hywel. Then a shaft of light shone down on Hywel, and a voice said 'Hywel Jones – you are the disciple'."

The ducks were totally absorbed with his story.

Jimmy felt rather pleased with himself as he went to the shop to buy his paper, but the feeling of self-satisfaction began to wear off. By the time he got home, he thought *that was rubbish. That's the way Walt Disney would have written it, and life isn't like that – and it's been done a thousand times and made no difference. In any case, I'm no hero, and I'm certainly no magician.* He turned to his newspaper, but that was worse. He flicked past one story after another; none of it seemed to have the same meaning any more. He could just see the newspaper was sensationalising, over-dramatising, and the real baddies behind the stories were getting off scot-free.

Though Jimmy did become something of a local hero for a while when news of the bear saga at the wedding got back to the Duck House.

"I wouldn't have gone out," said Jack.

"I did," said Billy, "Me and Dimitri went out to look for it."

"Yeah, half a mile behind!"

"It was no big deal," said Jimmy, "The bear was a friend of mine."

Jack and Billy looked at each other.

"What?"

"Yeah… but he'd gone when I got there." He saw the look on their faces. "I was as shocked as anybody else that the bear was there. I wasn't expecting him."

"What are you on about, Jimmy?" said Billy, "I suppose the chicken was a friend of yours as well, was he?"

"She. Yeah… Prima Donna."

"You've had a more colourful past than I thought," said Jack, "These friends of yours, known them for long?"

"Yeah. Well, forty days – and a bit extra if you count the extension."

Billy decided to go along with him, curious to see where this was going, "Prima Donna, eh? And Bear? I didn't know them,

Jim – you should have introduced me. Do they live round here?"

Jimmy was miles away. "Er, yeah… no… Milton Keynes, I think – you know, near the Wilderness."

Billy looked at Jack, "He's been at Daisy's pills again."

Jimmy snapped back into the present reality, "Ah! Had you going there for a bit, didn't I!"

"You did. Fair play," said Jack.

"You didn't believe him, did you?"

"No, course not, but weird stuff does happen. I haven't told anybody this, but a couple of years ago my old lady was in hospital. We knew her time was up, she wasn't coming out. Anyway, I'd heard about this book called The Art of Dying, or something, never read it, but this feller – a doctor, I think – had studied hospices, you know, the places that care for the old people. Well, the carers, some of the carers, after somebody had died they said they'd seen someone come and collect them – you know, from the other side. Anyway, apparently," he said, "if you can be, try to be there at the point they snuff it – and it could be up to an hour after death…"

"Where did you hear all this?" said Billy.

"It was on the telly, one of those obscure channels – can't remember. So, anyway, I got the hurry up call from the hospital about two o'clock in the morning. It took me over an hour to get there because I was living in North Wales at the time, and when I got there she'd gone – she'd been dead about an hour. Anyway, they let me go and sit with her – they were pretty decent at the hozzie. They brought me a cup of tea, and some biscuits… I used to do a bit of meditation a while ago – still do…"

"What? You do meditation?" said Billy.

"Yeah, Mickey Mouse stuff. This woman taught me – you know when I was doing the boxing? It works… it's good. Anyway, I'm trying to meditate, sitting in the chair, and she's lying there. My head was all over the place, took me ages. Then

I saw my old feller come in – and he died twenty years ago – but he wasn't alone. My grandfather was with him – you know, her old feller – and he died when I was a kid, but I remember him. I could see them, as clear as I can see you two, and I'm watching them walking down the ward, I could see them walking towards the bed. My old feller just goes over and picks the old lady up and carries her away, and my grandfather comes and shakes my hand… you know, with both of his. Then they both left."

"Bloody hell!" said Jimmy.

Billy just stared in silence.

"…So nothing surprises me any more. Anyway, meditation, Billy. I was telling Jimmy the other day, when I was doing a bit of boxing there was a poofter, you know, at the gym. He taught me a lot – couldn't put him down – he just wouldn't give up. Anyway, meditation – have a go, strengthens the old noggin. Right, I'm going to get the ale in. And by the way, if anybody else calls you a poofter, tell me."

* * *

It was a tad ironic: Mr Hargreaves and Mr Evans, Sinead's teachers, had made strenuous efforts, particularly Mr Evans, to persuade Sinead to continue with her education, yet it was they who left the school first. The official line was 'so as not to damage the school's reputation'.

After the wedding, the humour that was shared between Mr Hargreaves and Mrs Evans continued via the internet and led to clandestine meetings, which was inevitably doomed to failure with a school of five hundred pupils. After the divorces, Mr Hargreaves and Mrs Evans married, moved to Scarborough and bought a small guesthouse. The guesthouse was quite successful and quite fulfilling in a way, apart from the occasional guests who were totally unreasonable, and the disappearance of the odd towel or tea cup. To equalise this, of an evening they played 'Circus of Horrors', which meant emailing the perpetrators under various pseudonyms to see what buttons they could press. They convinced themselves there was nothing malicious or vindictive about it... Right.

The other half of the quartet also became, for want of a better word, a couple. Mr Evans was the one who had tried hardest to persuade Sinead to continue with her education, his argument being 'you can't go through life just doing what you want to do'.

There was no love in this relationship; their liaisons were more *sorties* rather than romantic candlelit dinners. Still, they too eventually got married, following the premise 'it would be better to make two people unhappy rather than four'. Mr Evans always wanted to retire to a cottage in North Wales... so didn't.

* * *

Jack, Billy and Jimmy were in the Duck House talking about the forthcoming football season.

"That was a weird story about your old lady," said Jimmy when there was a lull in the conversation, anxious to know more, "D'you believe something happens when we snuff it?"

"Do now. Probably always did, though I didn't give it a lot of thought. It's the only thing that makes sense."

"Must have helped you come to terms with it, though – you know, the old girl?"

"Yeah, course. But it was my grandad being there. He was a good man, by all accounts, he was a Methodist lay preacher, you know, part-time. I saw that woman a few months later, you know, the one who taught me about meditation. Told her the story about the... you know, me old feller and that. She wasn't surprised. She said that sort of thing often happens, usually in times of stress – you know, like big time..." He looked at Billy,

"Did you ever come across any weird stuff? You were in the army, weren't you? Middle East?"

"Yeah, all the time. Though it didn't get talked about – wasn't macho, was it. Middle East… it was a load of crap. A lot of men cracked up, decent blokes. A lad in our group blew his fucking head off." Billy paused for an age. "And he used my fucking gun."

Jimmy looked horrified. "Jesus Christ! You never told me that!"

"Never told anybody."

"What happened?"

"Just told you – he blew his fucking head off. Don't know why he used my gun… still don't."

"Bloody Hell! So, what did the Army do?"

"Do!" he said mockingly, "Nothing! I go to the shrink, he spouts some shit about we're all there for the good of mankind, gives you a couple of happy pills, and you get on with it."

"Shouldn't have been there, should we," said Jack.

"No! Yanks shouldn't have been there, either. It was all about oil, wasn't it. The Yanks had it worse. Half of them finished up drug addicts. You could get hold of heroin easier than buying a Mars bar."

"Christ! Did you ever try it?"

"No, no way! It's a load of crap. I've learned more about it since I got back. D'you know who the biggest drug lord is in South America? …It's the CIA. And over one million have died in Afghanistan and around there through drug addiction. I wouldn't be surprised if the CIA had a hand in that… and they don't give a fuck if their own guys get caught up in it, so long as it doesn't affect the god… the Yankee Dollar." Billy looked at their shock and disbelief. "The facts are all there. All the Army chiefs and politicians are bloody well aware of it, but they turn a blind eye. They just don't want to know.

"Anyway, it doesn't matter whether there's any proof about the CIA. Nobody would take any notice anyway. But what we all know is that they would, wouldn't they. Look at the vets from Vietnam, how they were treated… Like scum.

"And look at the Falklands. We all watched the war being played out on the telly; our ships sailing thousands of miles, and how proud we were to be British, charging off to the other side of the world to protect a few sheep farmers. And what do we find out now? There's oil there. Well, surprise, surprise. No wonder the Argies wanted it."

Jimmy wasn't contributing much to this conversation, but was absorbing every word like a sponge. "How were you treated in the Army, you know, being erm… were there many in the Army, you know…?"

"Many what, Jim?"

"I think he means bananas, or sewing machines, don't you Jim?"

"Fucking gays, you twat!"

"O-oh… same as everywhere else, I suppose. What is it, one in ten, one in fifteen? I don't know. Keeps changing. Nah, it's alright. You've got to stand your corner, don't let them walk over you, but that's the same for everyone."

"You got a trade out of it, though, didn't you, Billy?"

"You got a lot more than that, didn't you, lad! What is it they say: what doesn't kill you makes you stronger. Anyway, you've done that. So I hear you're having Greek lessons now, smart-arse. What's the next career – Greek shipping magnate?"

"Yeah, that's the one. Jimmy's already made my first boat, haven't you, pal."

"Too right. Tricky things, though. But you've got to make sure there's a string on the front so I can haul you back."

* * *

Jimmy finished his sculpture with head and arm mended; nobody would ever know. Molly helped him make the leatherette pouch to hold the plant, but he had grossly misjudged the balance between the plant and the sculpture. It was way out. He kind of knew the plant would be heavier than the sculpture as it went along, but then he kind of also hoped there would be some sort of divine intervention.

He often went for long walks these days. That was where he thought of The Solution to the balance thing: he needed a thinnish branch that was heavier at one end than the other. He eventually found one, and it was perfect, far better than it would have been the way he'd originally planned it. *There is no situation that doesn't have a solution.* Then he corrected it: *There is no situation you can't turn to advantage.* He had a feeling of *déjà vu*: he'd thought that before, or somebody had said it before. Slowly, bits of his time in the Wilderness started drifting back.

While Jimmy was on one of his walks he met a neighbour walking her dog, and stopped to talk. Her dog, Hollie, was frozen with fear, shaking, as some young lads whizzed by on scooters. "Oh, she does that," the neighbour said, "She's terrified of the scooters."

Jimmy was so moved by this, he wrote a story called Hollie and the High Tree, about the adventures of a puppy who was terrified of scooters, and how the puppy learned to conquer her fears and became a superdog.

Jimmy wanted to tell Hollie the story. Fear is a terrible thing. He knew the story would help, but he never got the opportunity. He always did want to help anybody he could. *Surely everyone wanted to do that – leave the world a better place? But the world isn't a better place – it's shit. How can that be?*

He began thinking about when he was a kid, and they got their first telly, and how magic it was watching the cowboys and Indians, and the good guys always won. *But if the good guys always win, why…?*

What if the Indians were the good guys? They were there first. It was the cowboys who took their land away. So they're going to kick up, aren't they? And where are the Indians now? Hounded out of existence, or stuck on some reservation somewhere, what's left of them. I bet there's no oil there – they'd have made sure of that.

But then you can't blame the Yanks, after all they were just Europeans anyway, a couple of hundred years ago... half of them, anyway. It's the whole lot, the whole world. Greed, selfishness, bullying and men... always men. He recalled the conversation they'd had in the Duck House, about the Middle East, and then the Falklands War. *That was Thatcher. Margaret Thatcher took us there – if not on a lie, the full truth was never told... not always men. Just a few bullies in the world dictate everything, and we let them get away with it. If we're not part of the solution, we're part of the problem. Who said that?*

They should give Manhattan back to the Indians. Yes, that'll do to start.

Chapter 24

"Look at this, Mam! The bloody electric's gone up again! Every week there's something else. It seems to be getting harder and harder to manage, and I can't ask Jimmy for more housekeeping; he hasn't had a rise for ages, and last time I mentioned it he said Charlie Madden's talking about laying people off."

"Well I've still got a bit of pension, and the insurance coming in from your Dad."

"No, you've done enough… but I tell you what – I've been thinking of taking a part-time job, just to help out a bit. I've got time these days, you know since the wedding. Sinead looks after her own washing, and Terry's. And she keeps the loft spotless – have you seen it? She never kept her own room that tidy… You could get JJ's tea, couldn't you, you know if I get a part-time job or something, and I don't get back for four o'clock?"

"What are you thinking of doing? And what will Jimmy say?"

"Oh, he'll be alright. I can swing him around. He knows everything's going up. A lot of women work these days, you know when the kids are growing up. But I've been asking around; there's not much part-time work going on. I could try the supermarket, I suppose."

"What about them," Daisy nodded towards the box of clothes in the corner. "You're never going to wear all them. Sell them."

"What? To a shop you mean?"

"Maybe," she shrugged, "Or a stall in the market, or something. The shops'll be no good, they'll want them for nothing."

"D'you think they'll sell?"

Daisy shrugged again, which was about as much approval as Daisy was likely to give.

"They are good, aren't they." She went and got the box out. "Look at this one. And that one goes with that."

* * *

"Hun..? Hun… Me and me mam have been talking. I'm thinking of getting a stall at the market. You know, maybe sell some of the clothes – you know, the skirts and tops I've made… What d'you think?"

Jimmy looked horrified.

"You don't like the idea, do you?"

"No, no! I think it's a great idea. But 'Hun' – where the hell did that come from?"

"I thought it would put you in a good mood."

"Well I was in a good mood. The market's a good idea – but leave the Hun bit out, it makes me feel sick. Anyway, I'm going for a pint."

* * *

"How's the book coming on, Jimmy?" said Jack.

"Don't ask. Threw it in the bin – it was crap. But I've got an idea for a new one and it's brilliant."

"Go ahead then. What's it all about?"

"Well, you gave me the idea – or was it you, Billy? About the law of right and wrong, you know the instinct we're all born with – we know, don't we, if something's right or wrong."

"I don't remember saying that. Must've been you, Billy."

"No, no. Probably right, though. But nobody ever does it."

"No, I know, but it's there, though, isn't it? That's the point. We all know instinctively whether something's right or wrong or not, don't we. Doesn't matter whether we obey it or not… though I suppose it does actually.

"Anyway, in the book, which I've only just started, the law of right and wrong says the Indians were cheated into selling Manhattan for a pittance, and the law of right and wrong said they were ordered to pay compensation to the Indians… you know, like what it's worth now."

"I'm getting a headache," said Billy, "But carry on."

"Well, Wall Street crashes. They can't afford it. But then they have to… so they make an offer that makes every Indian on the reservation – what's left of them – multi-millionaires… but then the Indians refused it."

"So, what, the Indians go and live in Manhattan?" said Jack, "In the skyscrapers, firing arrows out of the windows half a mile up in the sky?"

"No, Jack… behave yourself!! That would be stupid. No, the law of right and wrong said that Manhattan would have to be put back to the way it was," said Jimmy with some exasperation, thinking that would be obvious.

"So, what? So they go and put teepees up in Central Park? But hang on a minute, Jimmy, Manhattan's only about ten square miles, or something. Hardly room for herds of buffalo sweeping majestically across the plains."

"Ah, well, smart arse… in my story the buffaloes are only small – they're only about the size of a guinea pig.

"Anyway, Molly's going to make our fortune; she's going to get a stall on the market and flog some of those clothes she's been making."

"Oh, aye?" said Jack, "What are they like?"

"Gypsy style. They're good. BoHo or something," he added.

"BoHo? What the bloody hell's BoHo?"

"Christ! Bohemian Romantic! Don't you know nothing about fashion?"

"Ah, well there you go, that's your style, isn't it, Billy? How d'you fancy that now you've come out the wardrobe?"

"Piss off!"

* * *

Molly's dream became a reality and she took a small stall at the market. Thursdays, Fridays and Saturdays. Daisy went with her most days, though she drew the line at wearing the clothes… but maybe one day – after all she was still a chicken. And Sinead helped out on a Saturday.

Daisy moved into Sinead's old bedroom, and her old room, the front room, became a sewing factory.

Jimmy finished his sculpture and it worked exactly as planned, the house plant rising very slowly as it required watering. That's the way life should be: in balance. He called the sculpture 'Harmony'.

Jimmy placed Harmony on the blanket chest in the front window of their bedroom. Then something strange happened: as Jimmy was looking out of the window the plant moved. It began turning slowly. He must have knocked it, he thought. The next time he made sure he hadn't touched the plant, and it moved again. He became fascinated by this; what made it move? Must have been the wooden floorboards. He crept towards it to eliminate that possibility, and it still moved. Must have been the heat of his body. But then, when the radiator was on under the window it never moved.

It didn't happen every time. He showed Molly. The plant moved a little, but not as much as it had on other occasions. She dismissed it as probably being the vibration through the floor, but Jimmy knew it wasn't that, it was something else.

* * *

The football season had started, and the big match was tomorrow night at Anfield against their arch rivals, Manchester United. Jimmy was in the Duck House with Jack, but Jack wasn't interested in the football.

"What are you doing these days, then, Jack?"

"I've gone back doing the central heating and plumbing stuff. I served my time as a heating engineer, you know, before I took up the boxing."

"What, gas boilers and that sort of stuff? Could have done with you twelve months ago when our boiler broke down."

"Why? What happened?"

"Oh, it just stopped working, packed up. Called British Gas. Cost me a bloody fortune."

"I could have told you that! British Gas – they're a rip-off, you know. I used to work for them… How much did you finish up paying?"

"Don't remind me! Nearly three grand, I think, in the finish."

"Jesus! I'm not surprised. I packed it in with them because of things like that. You know what they used to have us doing? We'd go out on a call, check the boiler out, and even though it could be repaired we were told to scrap it and tell the poor sucker it was no good. And every time we did that we got fifty quid off British Gas, and then the heavy gang would go in and con the poor sod into all sorts."

"Bloody hell! The gets! That three grand was our holiday money. That's what stuck me with a load of crap from the council. I told you about that, didn't I."

"Yeah, I know… anyway, that's why I packed it in. They're just conning the most vulnerable people. I couldn't be doing with it. I work for myself now. I can undercut British Gas by half and still make a decent screw."

"And that's British Gas! Supposed to be the backbone of British industry, isn't it. I wish I knew you were doing that twelve months ago. But it's not just the gas, is it, everything's just going up and up."

"Has Molly taken that stall in the market?"

"Oh yeah, she's tickled pink! Don't know if it's going to make any money."

"You've got a good'n in your Molly, haven't you. She understood all that council shit, didn't she."

"Yeah, she's alright… D'you think you'll find somebody else one day?"

"Have done. Did do. Six years ago."

"What happened?"

"Ah well, remember I said? It was about the time me and Annette were splitting up. I was a bit of an idiot. Thought I could walk on water. Going to change the world and the rest of it. Scared her, she couldn't cope – she pissed off."

"Where is she now?"

"Don't know. Tried to find her. Even got a private dick. He was no use."

"Well, you'll find somebody else."

"No. She was the one."

"It's weird, that, isn't it. D'you think there is just the one, then, Jack?"

"Yeah. It was her. And it went both ways. Only happens once, Jimmy lad. Take care of Molly. Anyway, I'll get the ale in," Jack stood up, "If I don't find her in this life, I'll find her in the next."

The feeling of *déjà vu* came rushing back. The world Jimmy thought he knew wasn't – it was just a facade, and everybody was part of it. Jimmy had never been one for talking about the lovey-dovey stuff, and he was sure Jack wasn't either, yet they did. And yet, amongst all the crap, he was now convinced that love exists and only happens once. But how could that be? What's the chances of meeting that one person in the whole world – unless it's not by chance? Was there another life after this one? …Was Jack right?

Billy came in and joined them.

"We've just been putting the world to rights, haven't we, Jimmy."

"Oh, come on! The world's never going to be right."

"Not if you don't try, it won't. It's just greed. You know everybody just wants more and more money, and they don't care where it comes from or who suffers along the way. You told us that with the Yanks in the Middle East."

"Well you're right about that – the Yanks are the worst. Certainly wants changing. It's a load of crap."

"Don't forget the Yanks were all Europeans a couple of hundred years ago."

"Yeah, you've got a point there, but it'll take a miracle. Any good at miracles, Jimmy?"

"Yeah, I can do that."

"Good. We might need one tomorrow night, the way United performed last season."

"Oh, don't worry about that, lad – it's in the bag. Two-one, I tell you."

* * *

So came the evening of the football match. For the time being, Jimmy put aside all the problems of the world – nothing pulled rank over Liverpool FC. They were going to win 2-1. He knew that.

But they didn't. They lost, 2-1. He felt his whole world had collapsed. He'd been so sure they were going to win.

"Come on, Jimmy, let's go for a pint."

"No, not tonight – I feel sick."

How could Billy go for a pint? he thought, though they always went for a pint after the match, win or lose, but tonight he couldn't. Beaten 2-1 by their arch-enemy. That should never have happened.

The next morning Jimmy got to the shop to buy his paper, meet Billy and get the bus to work as usual. The headlines on the back page: BRILLIANT WIN BY LIVERPOOL 2-1. SUPERB GOAL BY GERRARD IN INJURY TIME. He went back in the shop to look at the other papers. The same.

By the time Billy arrived, he felt sick. He knew what had happened, he was there, and yet…

"Look Billy, I don't feel too good. I don't think I can go in today."

"What's up?"

"Oh, just a bit of a bug."

Chapter 25

Jimmy walked around the lake twice. He knew Liverpool had been beaten by Manchester United; he'd watched the game. And yet Liverpool won, 2-1. He found himself walking past the church where Sinead had got married. The priest saw him.

"Hello. Jimmy Downie, isn't it?"

"Oh, yes Father," surprised at him remembering his name.

"You look like you could do with a friend. D'you want to come in and have a talk?"

"Oh, no, Father, thank you. I haven't been in church for a long time. Well, apart from…"

"Well, why not come in anyway, just have a sit down. There's nobody there, apart from the cleaner, Mrs Kennedy. She won't bother you. Come on."

Jimmy followed him in and sat in one of the pews near the back. He knelt down and prayed. All his time in the Wilderness was now as clear as crystal. He'd been given this enormous task and it scared the life out of him.

He hadn't been in church for a very long time. He got disillusioned when, as a kid, he was forced to sing 'Jesus wants me for a sunbeam'. *No way,* he'd thought, *they don't know me.* But now that was exactly what was happening. He tried calling Voice in a loud whisper, but no reply. Was there a god? Is there a god? The whole world seemed to think so, and yet they all fight about it. There was certainly something going on. But why me? What am I supposed to do about it? He'd never prayed in his life before, but now he was.

He stayed kneeling for a long time, occasionally wiping a tear from the corner of his eye. Eventually the priest came up to him, "Mrs Kennedy has made some sandwiches. You must be hungry. Why not come and join me? Come on."

Jimmy followed.

"Look, here we are. Salmon and cucumber, and Mrs Kennedy has made some cake. Come on, tuck in. I've had mine."

The priest carried on with his business, so as not to force Jimmy into conversation. The sandwiches were good. *We don't have salmon,* he thought, *We can't afford salmon.*

The priest was doing his accounts. A couple of phone calls; one to his builder asking him how he could improve his quote, and one from someone Jimmy assumed was his boss, on how he was intending to raise money over the next quarter.

"Money, always money," said the priest as he put the phone down, as if he was reading Jimmy's thoughts.

The priest sat down. "Sometimes, Jimmy, when it's impossible to push water upstream you can get the same result by helping it on its way."

Jimmy left the church with the mouse in his head – not dead from exhaustion – but beginning to turn its wheel slowly, and gradually getting quicker and quicker. Running over and over in his mind was Voice saying 'a fool and his money are soon parted, but it's a bigger fool who's frightened of letting go of it.' That, and a thousand and one other things that Voice had said.

* * *

By the time Jimmy got back to the lake, the wheel was racing. Even the ducks noticed the remotivated Jimmy, and were pleased to see the familiar face again. He walked round the lake slowly, the ducks following at a short distance. He sat down on the bank at the edge of the lake and began to talk to the ducks.

"The world is full of greed, isn't it."

"Quack."

"I mean really full of greed,"

"Quack, quack…"

"Now bear with me on this, because I'm still kicking the ball around."

"Quack."

"The world is obsessed with a lust for money, isn't it."

"Quack, quack."

"And the only thing that obsession wants is more and more money, isn't it."

"Quack-ish."

"Oh, come on! You've got to agree with that."

"OK. Quack."

"And they don't care where the money comes from, so long as they've got it and so long as it keeps coming."

"I'm getting a headache, but Quack."

"OK, nearly there. So if everybody spends all their money and can't borrow any more, what's going to happen?"

"I want to go to the toilet."

"Well, wait a minute. The financial system'll crash, won't it – the whole world will crash, and the world will become a wilderness again… and we can start all over again, can't we."

There was an uncanny silence, a stillness, then the temperature in the lake rose a little as all the ducks had a good pee, then waltzed around the lake in a magnificent ballet celebrating the dawn of the New World.

Jimmy had walked around all day, and it was getting near to the time he would be expected home. He went to a pub on his way back, one where he was not really known, so he could put out some of the fire burning inside him before he, too, blew up.

All I've got to do is convince people to spend money, and they love doing that. The economy picks up because people are spending, businesses expand, more jobs, banks are happy so lend more money… more money… more money. Keep feeding the monster. Then stop, and it all blows up. No more greed, no more corruption, back to the wilderness – perfect.

But, despite how perfect it was, it wasn't putting out the fire. There was something else, something bigger, much bigger.

Molly had had a very similar day. She wasn't aware that Jimmy hadn't gone to work, but she knew there was something up, and it bothered her. She tried to get lost in her sewing, but it wasn't really helping. She put all her sewing away and started doing her accounts, but they weren't helping either, not in the way she was hoping. By the time she'd paid the rent on her little market stall, and materials, and this and that, there was little left. Maybe enough to pay for the electric bill, but that was about it. But she stuck with it, determined to make it work. *If I can concentrate on the stuff that is selling, and not waste any material, not try to make every single thing different from the one before – that would help.*

Her motivation for all this was another holiday for the family. That was the plan. Not now, not tomorrow, but soon. But, despite all her efforts, soon would never be soon enough. Pay the electric bill, but no way pay for a holiday. But then she had a brainstorm. *What if we… Maybe if we…?* She made herself a cup of tea while the brainstorm worked its way through, then got ready and went out.

On the way back home, Jimmy went back to the church to see the priest and asked him if it would be possible for him and Molly to renew their wedding vows. He discussed it with the priest for a few minutes; just a small affair, no guests, just a simple ceremony for him and Molly. The priest understood immediately and willingly agreed and, as it was just a simple ceremony, he could fit it in within a few days.

By the time Jimmy got home he was feeling much happier with the world. Why, he wasn't sure. His plan was brilliant in its simplicity, and it was big, very big. But first he just needed to pick the right moment to tell Molly about his idea of renewing their vows.

He was smiling when he entered his house, greeted by Molly, who was also smiling. They could have been looking in a mirror, each one dying to share the reason for their joy with their beloved.

Jimmy sat down at the table and Molly poured him a cup of tea. On the table were holiday brochures. Jimmy stared as Molly fanned them out.

"We can't afford another holiday!"

"Er, well, perhaps we can."

"Don't be soft! We haven't even paid the electric bill yet."

"Er, well, erm…. I was thinking… that maybe we could do with a new kitchen."

"A new kitchen! What are you on about?"

The mouse on Jimmy's wheel had been trotting quite merrily on the way back from the pub. It now froze, waiting for instructions.

"We can't do that!"

Molly flicked through the brochures. He could see her mouth moving, but no sound was coming out.

He repeated, "Can't do that!" but then heard himself say, "What, back to Corfu? No, can't do that. Can't do that."

"Well, I thought maybe Spain this time," Molly showed Jimmy a brochure.

Jimmy's mouse grew a pair of horns and started going round the wrong way. *It is spending money,* he thought, *Doesn't matter whose money it is. That's the plan, and it's a brilliant plan.* "What, the Costa del Plonka?"

"Yeah…" Molly nodded.
Moments later they were dancing around the living room,
"Oh, we're off to sunny Spain!
Viva Espana!
And the Council's paying once again!
Viva…"

* * *

The room went black. Silent. Then a bright light beamed down on Jimmy and a voice boomed out,
"JIMMY DOWNIE!"

Chapter 26

As the light returned, Jimmy was sitting on a boulder, his head buried in his hands. He knew he was back in the Wilderness but was too scared to face it, to face Voice. He knew the kitchen thing was wrong; he shouldn't have let Molly talk him into it. How could he do that, after all… How was he going to explain it to Voice… and Bear… and Prima Donna? Had he learned nothing?

He slowly lifted his head and dared to look; there was a mist, a fog. It was different. It was all different. He strained to see through the murk. There was smell of decay in the air. He struggled to his feet, stumbled and looked down. He hadn't been sitting on a boulder, there was just a pile of bricks. As the mist slowly cleared, he could see this was not the Wilderness he was familiar with, and yet he recognised it. He looked around, trying to focus through the murk. All he could see was decay and dereliction; houses boarded up, windows broken. No sign of life anywhere. He was standing at the bottom of his own street.

Jimmy looked back down the street to where his own house was and walked slowly towards it. He stared in horror. His house was in the same state as all the others: dark, dingy, window broken, the front door slightly open, but he was too terrified to walk in.

It's just a dream, I'm just dreaming, it's just a nightmare, he tried to convince himself.

He staggered down the street in a daze, telling himself *it's just a dream, it'll go away, it's just a dream, it's just a dream.* Past the Duck House. That was the same, derelict. He thought of knocking on the door, but he was too scared. The streets were deserted, cars abandoned, rusty, as if they'd been there for a hundred years. He walked on to the lake. That was no more: overgrown, unkempt, the lake practically dried up, the ducks gone.

He tried to call Voice, but there was no reply. The dream wouldn't go away... *What if it's not a dream... What if...*

"Now you're getting it."

"Voice! Voice! Is that you, Voice?"

"Are you expecting someone else?"

"Yes. No. I mean... I'm just dreaming."

"No, no, you're not dreaming. This is it. This is what you wanted, isn't it. Anyway, I'll let you get settled in... absorb the atmosphere, as it were. Or lack of it."

"What d' you mean? What's happened? ...Voice..." There was no reply. Jimmy called Voice several times. No reply.

This is what I wanted, he said. "No, no, Voice. I didn't mean this. Where's my family? I didn't mean this."

Was this the world he had created? The wilderness he had longed for just a few minutes ago was *this*? Was it just a few minutes ago? Hours? Days? Time meant nothing. *No, it's just a dream.*

But where was his family? Where was Molly? He tried calling her, "Molly! Molly! Where are you?" No reply.

"A good question – I was wondering that."

"Is that you, Voice? Voice? What's happened? Where's Molly? Where's my family?" But he was back on his own again.

He tried to walk, but couldn't. He was in such pain. The pain he felt was so strong he couldn't think of anything except Molly and his family. He collapsed in a heap and sobbed and sobbed. It seemed like he was there for an age.

The pain wasn't in his head.
It wasn't a headache.
It wasn't in his stomach.
It wasn't a stomach ache.
It was deep inside.
But not inside his body.
It was inside him.

If my family's gone, if they've all gone, I want to go too.

"Ah, well, no. That wasn't part of the plan."

"What?"

"The plan. Your plan. Brilliant in its simplicity, you said. Remember?"

"I didn't mean this!"

"I must admit it was a bit radical. But radical is what He asked for, and your plan was certainly radical. Anyway, there we are."

"But I didn't mean this! I want to go back! Take me back. I know the kitchen thing was wrong."

"Aah, no, 'fraid not. No backsies. No, no, doesn't bear thinking about. Just think about it: mending the windows in the Duck House, refurbishing the cars, filling the lake – the list is endless. Doesn't bear thinking about."

"Where's Molly? Where's my family?"

"Don't know. You tell me – it's your plan."

"But I didn't mean this!"

"No, so you said."

"I meant just get shut of the bad guys, the evil, the corruption, the greed."

"Yes, that's what we thought you meant. So that comes under the 'letting he who is without sin cast the first stone' category or, to quote yourself, the law of right and wrong."

Jimmy struggled to come to his senses. "If it's my plan, it's not the tiny, tiny bits of wrong that are wrong – it's the big bits of wrong that are really wrong."

"Right. And who decides which is tiny-tiny, and which is really-really? Which reminds me of Mayor Giuliano when he wanted to clean up New York; he said 'corruption has gone beyond an *acceptable* level'. One of my favourite quotes, that, but which has turned out to be a little academic considering the skyscrapers are currently being pulled down to make way for the Indians. Oh, and by the way, speaking of Indians, your idea of buffalo the size of guinea pigs has really caught on – everybody's getting them these days as pets, they're really cute. In short, who decides what is the acceptable level of baddyness? Though Mayor Giuliano did have a point… anyway, I'll let you sort that out."

"Giuliano… Buffaloes… buffaloes the size of guinea pigs… What are you on about?" Then he recalled the conversation he'd had with Jack and Billy in the pub just a couple of nights ago. "I only said that a couple of days ago."

"I told you before, time doesn't work like that. Remember? But don't worry about it – you'll understand one day. Anyway, they're really cute."

"What?"

"Oh yeah, they've become quite the big thing for Chrissie presents. But some of the buffalo are not being looked after properly, and they're being abandoned. So they've started a campaign: 'a buffalo is for life, not just for Christmas', but then that got taken over by another campaign: 'a buffalo's not just for Christmas, but for sandwiches on Boxing Day and then a curry'… You don't look very happy, Jimmy."

"I'm not. I feel terrible. No more Christmases."

"Of course there'll be more Christmases."

"You have Christmas up in heaven?" muttered Jimmy with his head buried in his hands, then realised it was a stupid question. "Oh, of course you do, Birth of Christ… Sorry, Voice, I'm not thinking straight."

"What?"

"Jesus Christ… Christmas Day… born on Christmas Day."

"What… Was he? Oh, so he was! So that's where the Christmas name came from! Oh, I just thought that was a coincidence. Well, doggone! Though I suppose I should say buffalogone now… You still don't look very happy, Jimmy?"

"I'm not. Has my family gone to heaven?"

"I don't know. I told you, it's your plan. You tell me. Look, got to go now. You've given me a problem – or, rather, just pointed out a potential one."

"Don't go! How am I going to change the plan?"

"Well, think about it. You believed you had the solution.

That's what got us here. So all you've got to do is believe you have another solution."

"Don't go! Don't go! What's the solution?"

"It's not up to me; it's up to you. Just remember, the power of belief is pretty, well… powerful. Anyway, got to dash now… Erm, why don't you go and find your little round boat?"

"What?"

"The coracle, Jimmy. The coracle."

"VOICE!   Voice!   Voice?"

Chapter 27

"Molly! Molly! Where are you?"

He tried to sit down, but he couldn't move, as though all his senses were frozen. The dried-up lake that stretched out in front of him was just a hazy blur... silent, deathly silent. He tried to sit again, but then realised he was already sitting. He closed his eyes and tried to focus on the lake and bring it back to the way it was, but he couldn't. His mind was racing like the demented ping-pong ball. He kept his eyes closed for an age, but very slowly he began to relax and feel calm. *There's no situation you can't turn to advantage. There's no problem that doesn't have a solution. How can death be turned to advantage? Unless... unless death doesn't exist – it's only the body that dies. The soul, whatever that is, doesn't. The pain I'm feeling isn't physical; it's the soul, the heart... No, it can't be the heart – that's just another organ.* Through his pain, Jimmy made himself chuckle. *What would happen with a heart transplant? Would you start loving someone else's missus?*

That's crap! That's crap! It's not the heart, he kept repeating it. *That's just a label we stick on it. The real pain – the real joy – has nothing to do with the body. It's got to be something else.*

You don't love somebody with all your heart; you love somebody with your soul, and the soul, whatever it is, is not supported by the body. So it doesn't need the body... so it doesn't need the body. Come on, Jimmy... it doesn't need the body. Come on, Jimmy, keep at it – you're nearly there.

He felt the enormous burden begin to lift. He slowly opened his eyes; everywhere was white. He rubbed his eyes but it made no difference. Just white. Not like snow white, just blank white. No sky, no lake, no grass, as though an artist had just drawn him in the middle of a piece of paper – but his fear had gone. He knew he was on the verge of something massive.

"Oh, that's tidy, Jimmy. Well done! Good lad!"

"But where is everything? It's all white."

"Yes, I thought it was alright."

"I didn't say alright! I said it's all white! I mean blank... nothing. Have I gone blind?"

"No, no... you're not blind. Perhaps you're seeing things for the first time – a clean sheet, as it were. Start again. That's what you wanted isn't it?"

"What!!" Jimmy's mind started racing again.

"Oh, by the way, I completely forgot. I just remembered when I got back... oh, and by the way, thanks for telling me about the Christmas thing. That could have caused us a problem..."

"What are you on about?"

"Christmas. That's a christian thing, isn't it. I told you we look after all the religions, you know, muslims, hindu, red indians, aborigines – they all amount to pretty much the same thing. But Christmas is a christian thing, and we can't be seen to be siding with one religion more than the other. You can see that, can't you. So anyway we've got to change the name. I suggested Buffalo, Happy Buffalo. I quite like the sound of that – what d'you think?"

"What the hell are you on about? What's all that got to do with me?"

"I'm getting there, I'm getting there. Don't get tetchy! I thought you'd be interested, seeing as it was you who brought buffalo into it. Well anyway, I remembered while I was away, you haven't played your Get Out of Jail card."

"What the hell's that got to do with it?"

"Right. Well, what it means, young Jimmy, is you can, if you want to – only if you want to, mind – you can play your Get Out of Jail card which means you can go back, right back to the beginning, and wipe the slate clean, as it were. So what d'you think?"

"I don't know what you're on about."

"Oh. Right, OK. Sorry. I'll explain. If you play your Get Out of Jail card you go right back to the beginning, you know, when you arrived at the airport on the way to Corfu, and I said 'You're the disciple' and you thought I said 'trifle' – funny, that – so you can wipe all that out. That doesn't happen. You still go to Corfu, but no lilo coming out of the sky. No old man with donkey – well, he'll still be there, actually – but no mysterious shortcuts, no salad. No two fishes and five loaves doo-dah. No match fixing – all your memory of all that will be gone."

"What – no wilderness, no Bear, no Prima Donna?"

"No, that's right. No… and Man U. win 2 – 1. But! But! If you don't play your Get Out of Jail card you'll go through everything exactly the same all over again without any memory whatsoever of it already having happened, if you see what I mean."

Voice paused for a long time to let Jimmy think that through. "So, in a nutshell, two choices:

"One, you go back to the airport, you play your Get Out of Jail card and you go off to Corfu – without the Disciple stuff – no Wilderness, no Prima Donna, no Bear – all that's gone; or

"Two, you go back to the airport, you become the Disciple, and everything will be as you remember it – though you won't remember it – everything that happened will happen again: Bear, Prima Donna, loaves/fishes thing, and you beat Man U. It'll be as though it's all happening for the first time – until we get to where we are now. But now, and this is the biggie, you haven't got your Get Out of Jail card. That's gone. And you take it from here.

"So, there we are. Let me know what you think, and I'll see you later – or not, as the case may be."

"Oh, I can tell you right away! Voice! Voicie..? VOICIE!" he shouted again, louder. But nothing. The sound just echoed back.

"Well, I'm not going through all that again!"

"Coracle… oracle… what the hell's he on about?"

"Change the bloody world? Get shut of the crap?"

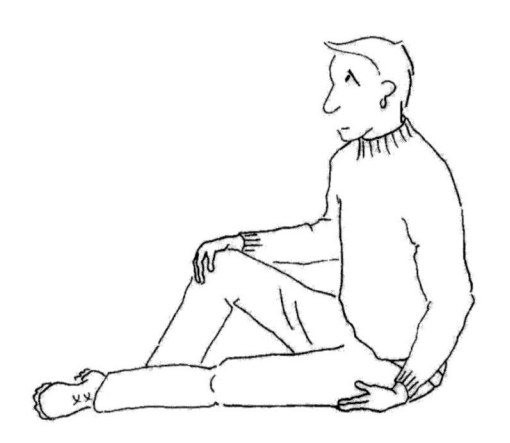

"…and me… why me?"

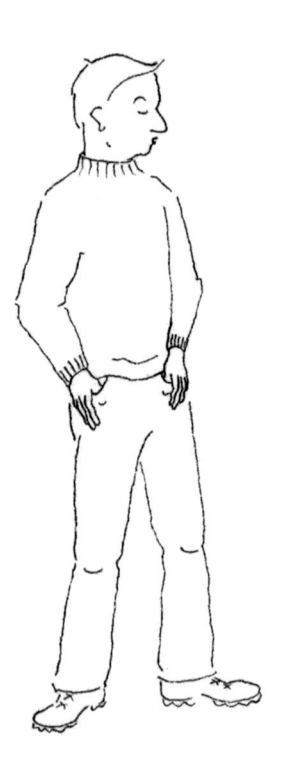

"I mean…"

"Bloody hell, Voicie!"

Chapter 28

A jet was making its approach. "Is that our plane, Dad?"

Jimmy stared into the sky.

"Probably lad... Cosmic." His mind was way beyond the planes.

"What's cosmic, Mam?"

"That's best known to yer Dad. Here lad, come here. Help me carry this."

There was an air of nervous anticipation as they approached the entrance. None of them had been abroad before, or on a plane before, apart from Sinead who went to Switzerland with school two years ago, but that gave her the edge over the others.

"Right, we have to look for the big board with all the departures on... there it is..." But that was as far as she got. Her voice stopped mid-sentence. Then everything went black, jet black, just for a moment. When the light returned, the airport was still, silent, frozen in time, as if someone had pressed the pause button... apart from Jimmy.

He nudged Molly, "What the hell was that?"

But she couldn't hear him, didn't move, frozen like a statue looking at Sinead. Sinead was the same, pointing towards the departures board. He saw a man in uniform, a pilot. He walked over, "What was all that about?" But nothing. The whole airport was still, silent, nothing, and nobody moved.

Then he heard a noise, a voice, a whisper, quiet, as though not to disturb anyone, "Jimmy Downie."

He looked around to see where it came from.

"Jimmy. Jimmy Downie," the whisper grew louder.

It appeared to be coming from above, but it could have been from anywhere.

"Jimmy!" The whisper louder still, a bit impatient.

"Hello?" said Jimmy, nervously.

"At last! Jimmy Downie – You are THE DISCIPLE."